For the Smiths,
with all good wishes,
David D. Anderson
Port Clinton
April 16, 1994

ROUTE 2,

TITUS,

OHIO

by
DAVID D. ANDERSON

Editor: Carol Spelius
Lay-out editor: Wayne Spelius
Staff assistant: Anne Brashler

Cover Artist: Susan Mirow

LAKE SHORE PUBLISHING
373 Ramsay Road
Deerfield, IL 60015
(708) 945-4324

ISBN # 0-941363-26-0
copyright 1993
price: $7.95

Foreword

David Anderson, author of ROUTE 2, TITUS, OHIO, has created a gripping tale. He is in touch with the earth and its tenders. He also knows how to write.

This combination of authority, experience, talent and imagination has created a compassionate novel concerning a farm family in Ohio after World War II. He brings to us a revelation. You'll not forget these people he has created. You will grieve for them, long after you've finished reading.

Chapter 1

I always liked to go in to Titus by myself and look around when Ma wasn't along to hurry me and to tell me to do things like get a haircut, so I was glad that the train was late. I stood by the station and watched a switch engine for a while and talked to a fellow who worked there. I told him about me coming in to town to meet my brother Johnny, who was coming home from the army, and he told me that lots of fellows were coming home now that the war in Europe was over, and I'd better look sharp when the train came in or I might miss him.

I could tell he was kidding because he was kind of grinning like a lot of the folks in Titus did when I came in, but I didn't say anything except that I wouldn't miss him. The man laughed and then went inside the station. I stayed there, watching and hoping that I'd know Johnny when I saw him.

I knew I would, though, because he was so much taller than me or almost anybody, and I couldn't help but remember how he laughed, and I knew he'd be laughing when he got off the train. Besides, he'd have a girl with him, his wife, he said in his letter. He married a girl that he'd met at camp, and he sent her picture. I looked at the picture once in a while the last few days, where it was put up .pa on the sideboard, and I figured I'd know her even if I didn't know Johnny. But I knew I would. After all, he was my brother.

The train came in then, a long one with one of the new engines pulling it. The engine stopped right in front of me. I felt like watching it because I like engines, but I walked on down by the passenger cars to watch for Johnny. Four or five people got off, and then I saw him. He saw me, too, and waved. He sure looked good in his uniform. He was grinning. I ran down the platform.

"Hi, Bobby." He grabbed me by the arm. "How are you, kid? Where's Ma and Pa?" He was laughing, like he always did.

"They're home. I come in by myself."

"You? You old enough to drive?"

"Sure. I got my own pickup truck." He always did make me feel kind of little. I don't mean in size or age or anything, and I could feel myself getting kind of mad. I didn't want to.

"Of course he's old enough, Johnny." It was a girl speaking. She'd been behind him, and I didn't see her before, but now she came up beside him. She looked pretty small beside him, but she was almost as tall as me. She was smiling at me.

"Hi. If Johnny won't introduce me, I'll have to do it myself. I'm Stella. Your new sister."

"Hi." I didn't know what else to say, so I stood there looking at her. She had long, wavy black hair, and her skin looked kind of tan, darker than any of the girls around Titus or at school. I remembered Pa saying something about pretty Goddamn fancy when Ma read him the letter, just because of her name, but I didn't pay much attention. Now I knew. And she was really pretty.

Suddenly Johnny squeezed my arm till it hurt. "Come on, kid. Show's over. Don't stare like the rest of the yokels." He let his hand drop, and as I turned away I saw the smile leave Stella's face.

"Johnny, don't do things like that."

"It's all right," I told both of them. "The truck's over behind the station." I started to walk away.

"Don't be in such a rush, kid. We've got some luggage if they ever get it off that thing."

"It can wait, Johnny," the girl said as I turned back to where they were standing. She was smiling again, and her voice was soft and even, not like most of the girls around here. I hoped she would say something else, and she did then.

Johnny gave a sudden, ugly laugh. "You won't see much." I looked at him quick, but his grin was the same. "Okay," he said to her. "if that's what you want."

"Truck's over here," I said again, and as I started to walk over, Stella took Johnny's arm. They walked a few feet behind me, and I could hear Stella's low voice. Then Johnny laughed again. It sounded mean. I'd almost forgotten how he could be sometimes. You can forget a lot in almost four years, especially if you want to.

I was going to open the door for them, but then I figured hell. Let Johnny open it. It was the least he could do. He got to go to the war and now he had Stella, and all I had was a worn-out truck. I was proud of it before, but now I could see that it was old and almost worn-out. I wished it was one of the shiny new Fords I'd seen in some of the magazines. It wouldn't be long before you could buy one, if you had the money. But I probably never would, I figured. It took me long enough to pay for this one.

Stella was already sliding across the seat when I got in, and then Johnny got in, pushing her over tight against me as he slammed the door. The glass rattled, but I didn't say anything as I started the motor and pulled out into the street. I sat over against the door, but I could feel Stella up against me. I looked straight ahead as I drove. Johnny's letter said she was eighteen, the same age as me, but she seemed lots older somehow, and I felt kind of nervous.

Johnny said something to Stella and she giggled. It made me feel like I shouldn't be there, like I wasn't wanted. As we turned off of Railroad Street onto the state road, Stella put her hand on my arm.

"You'll have to ignore us, Bobby. We've only been married two months, and Johnny had to be at camp most of the time."

"I will," I said, not looking at her. She let her hand drop and didn't say anymore.

I felt ashamed of myself. She was just trying to be nice and I didn't have to be mean. She was Johnny's wife, and it wouldn't cost me anything to be nice to her, too.

Nobody said anything for a while until on the outskirts of the town, when we passed the new high school building. I kind of wanted to tell Stella that's where I went for almost three years till I had to get a job and help the folks, but before I could, Johnny spoke up.

"There's Titus Consolidated High School," he said. His voice sounded bitter, but I don't think Stella caught it because I could feel her twist in the seat to look at it as we went by.

"It's a nice building, Johnny. It looks like it's cheerful inside, not like schools used to be."

"I wouldn't know. I never saw the inside of it. I went to the old one for a year."

"Oh," Stella said in a low voice, but Johnny didn't pay any attention.

"None of us Lusts ever had much use for schoolin'. Pa told us we didn't. And so did the teachers. And the nice parents who didn't want their kids sittin' too close to us."

"What do you mean by that, Johnny?" Stella's voice sounded kind of scared. "I never heard you talk like that before."

"Never mind. Don't pay any attention to me. You'll find out soon enough." There was the sharp snap of a match on his fingernail, and he lit a cigarette. "Just remember what I told you. You stick with me and you'll have more diamonds than you can carry. You won't have to worry about things like that."

"I never asked for diamonds, Johnny."

"You'll have 'em."

I didn't like the way Johnny was talking or the way his voice sounded, so I speeded up till we were going fifty. It was faster than I ever drove the truck before, but I wanted to get out to the farm in a hurry and get it over with. Maybe later, when Johnny got a job and got his old rifle out and got another hunting dog, he'd get the war out of his system and be all right. I read some place that there was bound to be trouble for a while, and I didn't want any part of it.

It was just six miles from the school out to the farm, and we made it in about ten minutes, with nobody talk-

ing and the motor sounding like a bucket of bolts and
Johnny smoking till my eyes started to burn. The farm
looked kind of pretty as we came up the hill, with the
new leaves out on the trees and the house with the red
siding that looked like brick but wasn't, that Pa and I
had put on last fall when he was still working. I wished
it was as pretty up close, and I began to slow down.

"There it is," Johnny said suddenly as he dropped his
cigarette on the floor.

"Oh, it's pretty," Stella said as she leaned forward to
look. She put her hand on my knee, and I sort of
twisted it away as I put on the brake to turn into the
lane. I was kind of glad she thought it was pretty from
the road, though.

I pulled up beside the house, just missing one of the
cats, and stopped by the kitchen door to let them out.
Johnny jumped out and then stood there until Stella
got down. Then he looked at me.

"Ain't you comin' in?"

"I got to put the truck away."

"Leave it out. I want to use it." His voice sounded
stern and I looked at him. Then I remembered he had
been a sergeant, and I felt kind of proud of him. I bet
he was a good one, the way his voice sounded. Still, I
didn't go for it much. He used to boss me before.

"I got to pick up the luggage, remember?"

"Oh." I turned off the motor and sat there watching
as he and Stella went in the side door. Stella glanced
down at the pile of old tin cans beside the pump and I
wished I had hauled them down to the gully like I'd
been intending to do.

After the door closed, I got out to check the oil. It was down a quart and I figured I'd better put some in if Johnny was going to drive. Still, I intended to tell him to take it easy. There was about a quart in a can in the back, and I poured it in, spilling a little down the side of the motor. Johnny was my brother and I was glad to see him and everything, but still I was a little nervous. I guess I was just jealous or something. I wasn't used to girls as pretty as Stella.

After I put off going in as long as I could, I wiped my hands on a rag and went inside. They were all in the kitchen, sitting around the table and talking. Johnny was just finishing telling Pa about something in the army, and Pa laughed. He hadn't shaved although he'd said he guessed he would before we got back. Stella smiled a little, like she was tired, but Ma didn't seem to pay much attention. She just watched Johnny. I pulled a chair up beside Ma. I was afraid she'd get excited and get sick again, like she was before, but she seemed all right. As long as she didn't fret or anything, I figured she'd be okay.

After a few more minutes of Johnny talking and Pa laughing, Johnny pushed his chair back.

"Well, if I'm goin' to pick that stuff up and get back before supper, I'd better move." He looked at me. "You'd better show me how to run that contraption."

"I'll drive." I didn't want him messing with it, but I knew it was no use. He would anyway.

"No, you stay here and show Stella around."

I followed him to the door, and outside he turned to me.

"I can drive the damn thing all right. I can drive anything that's got wheels. I wanted to know if you've got any money."

"Not with me."

"Got any in the house?"

I nodded.

"How much?"

"Seventeen dollars. I been savin' to buy a tire."

"Get it. Don't worry. You'll get it back.

With interest."

I didn't want to, but I did, out of the cigar box that I kept in my room off of the kitchen. When I went through again on my way outside, Ma looked at me and smiled a little. I wondered if she knew what I went in for. I guessed she did. Ma could tell about things.

Johnny was sitting in the truck, with the motor running. He took the money and said "Thanks" as he put it in his pocket. I told him it was okay and then after he turned around and started to pull out, I walked down by the barn. I didn't want to watch him barrel down the hill and I didn't feel like going in just yet. Things seemed different already.

After puttering around among all the junk in the barn for about half an hour, I decided to go back into the house. Johnny would have been home by now if he was coming right back, but he hadn't showed yet and Stella would probably be worried. I was, too, because he was in such a hurry for my seventeen dollars. You'd think the army didn't pay him, and he wrote that he was making good money as a sergeant.

There was a pile of moldy old hay just inside the door that I kicked at as I went out. It reminded me why I was worried about Johnny. It was where the sheriff had found the guns and stuff from the hardware store when Johnny was sixteen, seven years ago. Pa hadn't said anything about it, only beat him, and I wondered if he still remembered it. Ma did, I could tell. She still worried about Johnny, even if she did like him best. I could see it in her eyes as she looked at him in the kitchen while he was telling his stories. Ma would do anything for Johnny -- except lie to the sheriff, she wouldn't. That's why he found the stuff in the barn.

I looked up the road for a minute or two, but the truck wasn't in sight. The sun was going down and it was getting chilly outside, so I went in, letting the door slam behind me. Ma was over at the stove, stirring something in a pot, and Pa and Stella were sitting at the table drinking coffee. Stella looked up quickly as I came in.

"Oh. Is Johnny back?"

I shook my head. "Not yet," I told her and pulled up a chair across the table from her and Pa.

Pa put down his cup. "Might take a while to get Charlie to open the baggage room. Usually have to pull him out of a saloon this time of day."

Stella nodded. She seemed a little lonesome and I knew why. Pa and Ma weren't much company if you weren't used to them. They didn't have much to say to each other and sometimes it seemed like they just forgot how to talk.

May came over to the table then, with a cup of coffee for me. "This'll hold you till supper. It's going to be a big one. I killed a chicken." She started to go back to the stove and then stopped. "You'll have to sleep on the couch here in the kitchen, son. Johnny and Stella are goin' to have the side bedroom."

I put sugar in my coffee, not saying anything, but it made me mad. I had all the stuff I'd collected in there and everything and now I wouldn't have any place to keep it. And Johnny would probably laugh and make me haul it out in the barn. It wasn't fair.

Stella got up then and went over to Ma. I heard her ask where the bathroom was, and I spoke right up. I was feeling mean.

"It's out next to the henhouse. And that's not what we call it," I said, as nasty as I could.

Her face was red, but she walked to the door, not looking at anyone. After she went out, Ma looked at me. I looked away.

"I don't want any trouble, Bobby. Johnny's home an' Stella's his wife an we got to make room. Please, I don't want any trouble. You got to be nice."

"You don't have to worry about me, Ma. I never give you any trouble." I said it so she'd know who I meant, but she didn't say anything, just turned to stir the pot on the stove. After a minute, I felt kind of ashamed. Pa was already nodding in his chair, so I drank my coffee and then went into the bedroom to take some of my stuff out of the drawers.

It took me a long time because I packed it carefully in some boxes that I had. Ma came and looked in once and said something about it being warmer in the kitchen during the winter, but I didn't pay any attention. Winter was a long way off. She went out then, and

I wished I'd said something nice. But I didn't know
what to say, and I guess Ma didn't expect it, anyway.

Chapter 2

Ma said she didn't want any trouble, and I sure
didn't either because I knew how Johnny could be, so
after I got my stuff packed away and before Johnny got
home I carried it out in the barn, a box at a time.
There were three boxes of stones I'd got down at the
quarry, all of them full of what Pa called "rock butter-
flies." I knew they were fossils though, and I figured
on buying a book and studying up on them some day.
Johnny would laugh and say I was nuts if he ever found
out, so I put them 'way back in a corner of the barn
where he'd never go.

It was pretty hot carrying the boxes, and when I got
through I sat down and took one of the rocks out to
look at. It sure was pretty, all full of fine veins and nets
and holes, just like lace made out of stone. Maybe if
Johnny would ever sit down and look at them like I
did, he wouldn't laugh. But Johnny never tried to study
things out. He'd either laugh or get mad. He always
laughed at me, and at school he'd get mad. And when
he'd laugh at me, Pa would too, and when he'd come
home from school mad, Pa'd nod and say "Damn right,
Johnny. You tell 'em." Ma would kind of frown, and I'd
sit there hating to go to school because I was Johnny's
brother.

I put the stone back in the box and closed it up, half
expecting the truck to pull up the lane and Ma to call
me for supper then. Even though Johnny had my truck,
I was kind of half wishing that he wouldn't come back.
I was glad to see him and all, but things had been

going fine while he was in the army, and Ma didn't worry so much, and I could do pretty well what I wanted to, go down by the old quarry or the river, or work on my truck since I got it, or anything.

Johnny wasn't always kind of hard to get along with, though. I could remember when he was thirteen or fourteen and I was just a little kid and we had a lot of fun together. There wasn't any other kids around the farm, and Johnny and I'd go for nuts in the fall, and we'd go swimming in the creek even though we'd have to lay down to get wet all over, and once in a while we'd go over in Bill Glen's pasture and plague his bull. Johnny laughed a lot then, but it was as much at himself as it was at me.

After Johnny got out of the eighth grade and started going to the high school in town, we didn't run around together so much. I was pretty much of a kid and he wasn't much interested in those things anymore. He started going to dances and went out for the football team and stuff, but still we got along all right. Then on Saturday, when it was starting to turn cold, I was out in the barn by myself.

Johnny'd been to a dance the night before and was still in bed, and I didn't want to make noise in the house so I went out to cut some boards. I was making a house for a dog Pa said a man had promised him for me. I figured if I made the house Pa wouldn't say he'd forgotten and the man gave the dog to somebody else.

I was getting pretty cold because I just had an old sweater on, and I was thinking about going in the house to get warm when Johnny came in the barn. He hooted as he came in.

"Boy, it's gettin' cold. Pro'bly snow tonight."

"How 'bout helpin' me hold this board, Johnny?"

"You still workin' on that old dog house?"

"Sure. I want to get it ready."

"Pa'll never get the dog. He was just talkin'. That's all he ever does, talk just to hear himself."

"If I make the doghouse, he'll have to get it like he said."

"If you want a dog, you better get it yourself. You never will if you wait for Pa."

Johnny just stood there, so I tried to brace the board so I could cut it, but my hands were too cold. I put down the saw and blew on my hands to warm them up a little bit.

"What's the matter, Bobby? Why don't you wear your gloves or something?"

"They're too little. I can't get 'em on anymore."

"Why don't you ask Pa to buy you a new pair?"

I didn't say anything, just went on blowing on my hands, but I wondered why Johnny said that. He knew Pa didn't have any money, not very much anyway, now that he wasn't working. He'd worked on the railroad section all summer, and then come home mad, saying the foreman's brother took his job.

"Why don't you, Bobby? Tell Pa you need some new gloves, and a pair of shoes while you're at it? Maybe you'll get 'em. Just like you'll get the dog, just like we'll get more than beans an' bread with lard on it. Just like I'll get some decent clothes to go to school in so the kids'll quit snickerin' when I go up the aisle. Or so I can go to a dance an' do more than stand around in a corner because the pants Ma cut down for me are too big in the seat."

"Johnny, don't talk like that. Pa can't help it. You know times are pretty tough. Even Bill Glen's hired man said so. He said Bill couldn't pay him."

"Bill Glen's still farmin', ain't he? An' they're still eatin' regular, ain't they?"

"Pa had to sell the stock 'cause the bank took the tools."

"That was years ago. I can't even remember it, and you can't either. You wasn't even born yet."

"Yes I was. Pa says I was. That's why it was so bad. Ma was sick a long time after."

"That's what Pa says. Ma never said nothin' about bein' sick."

"Let's not talk about it, Johnny. I guess I'll go in the house. It's too cold to work anymore." I was getting scared talking about Pa like that, and I felt funny inside. At the same time I kind of wanted him to go on talking. I'd never thought about Pa and the dog. Things like that had happened before. "Let's go in the house," I said again. I put my hands in my pockets and looked at Johnny. His eyes were red, and he rubbed them with his fists.

"What you lookin' at me for?" he yelled.

"Nothin', Johnny. W'd better go in." I started to go, kind of waiting for him to follow me, but he didn't move.

"Go ahead. Run in the house. Tell Ma what I said if you want. See if I care. Maybe Pa will get the dog an' some new gloves for you an' everythin' else. Go ahead," he yelled at me and then kicked the sides of the doghouse that I'd nailed together. A board split and a piece of it flew across the barn. "There, God-damnit, that's the way you'll get your dog an' everythin' else."

Johnny didn't get mad very often, but when he did, he really got mad. I was too scared to say anything, so I just stood there. In a minute he calmed down some and turned to me.

"I didn't mean to bust your doghouse, Bobby. I'll help you fix it, though." he kind of grinned then. "Guess I thought for a minute it was Pa. That's what he needs, a good, swift kick."

"It's okay, Johnny. I pro'bly won't need it anyhow."

"Sure you will. I'll get you a dog. Come on." He started to pick up the piece that he'd kicked. I just stood there, and he looked up at me.

"You ain't mad, are you, Bobby?"

"No, I ain't mad." I just felt tired and thought what was the use? I'd never get a dog anyway. Pa said they ate lots of meat, and we only had it ourselves about once a week.

Johnny went on picking up the pieces and started to whistle. After a minute he put them down in a pile and looked at me again."Look, Bobby, don't say anythin' about this, will you?"

"No. Why should I?" I listened to him talk about Pa, and that was just as bad. Ma always said lettin' others do things were just as bad as doing them yourself.

"I mean about what I said. Even if it's true. It is true, ain't it, Bobby?"

I nodded, and then he looked at the boards again, and started to push them around with his foot.

"We got to get better boards. A dog like we're goin' to get will need a first-class doghouse."

"Yeah. It's too cold to work on it anyway. We better go in the house, Johnny, before we catch cold."

We went up to the house then, and just before we went in, Johnny said, "I'm gonna go into town this afternoon. You want to go along?"

He'd never asked me before, although he'd hitch-hike in by himself once in a while, and for a minute I almost said yes, but then I said, "No. Ma prob'ly wouldn't let me anyhow."

After we ate, Johnny went in by himself, and that was the start of it, because that evening when he came home he came in the bedroom and shut the door. I was laying on the bed doing my lessons, waiting for supper. He pulled something out of his pocket and threw it on the bed next to me.

"Here, Bobby, I got you some gloves." He sounded kind of nervous, and I put down my book.

"Ain't you gonna try 'em on? If they don't fit, I can take 'em back." He laughed then, kind of mean, and I knew where he got them. I put them on then. They were thick brown cloth, a little long in the fingers.

"Want I should exchange 'em?"

"No. They're okay, Johnny. They fit pretty well."

"You ain't thanked me yet, Bobby," he grinned.

"Thanks, Johnny." I pulled them off and looked at them. I was scared because right away I knew Johnny'd stolen them. He went out in the kitchen then, and I put the gloves under the bed. I never put them on again, either, and one day on my way to school I threw them in the creek. Even then I was scared somebody would find them and know I had them on.

Johnny never said anything about me not wearing them, but he never brought me anything else, and after that we didn't do much or talk much together. Once in a while, though, I'd catch him looking at me kind of funny. About that time, too, he started calling me kid. He knew I didn't like it, but even yet he still kept it up, and I still didn't like it.

And now he was back, and he was my brother, and we'd have to get along. Maybe being in the army and being married would make him different. I got up to go into the house, feeling a little ashamed. I wished I hadn't made fun of Stella. After all, she was Johnny's wife. I threw some hay over my boxes, though. I still figured Johnny'd laugh if he looked in them.

As soon as I got outside, I saw the truck wasn't back. He'd been gone plenty long enough to bring back their luggage. I felt a little mad again, so I walked up as slow as I could. It was almost dark, and a few stars were out. Down at Bill Glen's I could see a tractor light in a field. They worked till late every night in the spring.

I remembered the trash then that I was going to carry down to the gulley, so I got a basket and loaded the stuff in. As I went around the house I stumbled on the pile of mud where Pa started to dig the summer before. It was where the septic tank was going to go. He said Ma and him were going to have inside plumbing in their old age. But that was a year ago, and Pa's back got bad after a couple day's digging, and a new crop of weeds was growing on the pile of dirt. I walked around the hole beyond and went down to the gulley. I wished for once that Pa would of done what he'd said. Then I couldn't of made that nasty crack to Stella.

So Johnny was back, I told myself on the way back after I dumped the trash. My brother was back from the war. I should feel pretty good. I could have something to brag about for a change. I could tell some of his stories to the kids in town, if they would listen. And they'd have to, because Johnny's stories would be good. He'd been a sergeant and all. I tried to tell myself it would be fun, that we'd tramp in the woods, and Stella would go along, laughing, and maybe we'd start to farm again and make it pay like Bill Glen did. Glen wouldn't like giving up the land he rented from Pa, but he would, and we'd make out pretty well. Then I came around the house and the truck wasn't back. I could smell chicken frying, and I remembered I was hungry, but it didn't seem to matter. I kicked the doorstep and hurt my toe as I went in the house.

Chapter 3

I had to work the next day, so I was up early. Ma woke me when she got up and then Pa came in. I kind of forgot about anybody else, but when I came in from washing at the pump, Johnny was sitting at the table with Pa, and Ma was serving him pancakes. He was joking with Pa, and Ma seemed happy, just as if he hadn't stayed out the night before until supper was cold and the biscuits were hard and Stella'd gone into the bedroom so we wouldn't see that her eyes were all red. He said he'd been talking business with a man and hadn't had but one beer, but had forgotten the time.

It smelled like more than one to me, but he put one arm around Ma and the other around Stella and said, "After all, I've got a wife to take care of, and you two, and even Bobby, if he'll let me," and that made it all right and everyone smiled and forgot the over-done chicken except me. And now he was up already this morning. Pa kind of frowned at me when I sat down, just as if I hadn't worked steady for almost two years.

"Johnny says he's goin' to start a junkyard." His mouth was full, and I could hardly understand him. "Says he wants you to work for him."

"I got a good job."

"Yeah, thirty-eight bucks a week. A real good job," Johnny said, laughing.

"It's enough for me. And it's been feedin' Ma and Pa, too, for over six months." I didn't like to say it, but I was mad. Johnny ignored it, though.

"You can make some real money with me."

"How? Sellin' junk? There's plenty of it around here."

"No. Used auto parts. Parts are hard to get, so we strip junk cars down and sell the parts. And when we get a car we can fix up, we do, and we can make a killin' on it."

The way he told it, it sounded easy, and for a minute I was tempted. But it would probably be like everything else he ever tried. He'd had at least ten jobs and been arrested twice before he ever went to the army. Besides, there were a lot of junkyards around, one not two miles down the road.

"No, I'm satisfied, Johnny."

Pa leaned back in his chair and belched. He still hadn't shaved. "If I was twenty years younger, I'd be in it with you, Johnny. Maybe you'll let me putter around a bit, anyway? I ain't much good with my bad back anymore, though." He sounded as though he was afraid of Johnny, and it made me a little mad. Ma brought my pancakes so I began to eat. I had to be at work before seven.

Johnny speared a piece of pancake with his fork. "We'll sure be able to use you, Pa, when the junkers start to come in. An' we'll have to clear all that old stuff out of the barn an' build racks for the parts. It's a good thing you never went much for farmin' or you'd have it cluttered up with animals."

"Now, Johnny, you know I did before things went to hell in '32. I farmed steady before then."

"Things were pretty good during the war."

"With a bad back, a man ain't much good. I worked in town for awhile, though, till they let me go."

"Hell, I didn't mean anythin' by it, Pa." Johnny turned to me. "What time you goin' in, kid?"

"Twenty to seven." I was still wondering who Johnny meant by we, but I didn't ask.

"It's pretty early, but I guess I'll have to ride along if I want to use the truck. Unless you want to quit and throw in with us."

"Who's us?" I tried to act like I didn't care.

"George Hite's goin' in with me."

I put down my fork. "He ain't even a good crook, Johnny. He's been in more trouble than you can shake a stick at, an' he never gets any smarter."

"He's all right now," Johnny said, and Pa nodded. "Besides, he really knows cars."

"He ought to. He spent three years in reform school, learnin' the trade."

"That's all over now. An' I got to have somebody who knows cars."

"There's lots of guys gettin' out of the army."

"George's got a little money, and he's been here to know the market. An' he's got connections."

"Yeah," I said sarcastically and began to eat again.

"The hell with you then. You can't say I didn't ask you." He didn't sound mad, though, and he laughed as he lit a cigarette and threw the match on his plate. I winced. Ma didn't like smoking. Still, she wouldn't say anything to Johnny.

She came over to the table then, with more pancakes. "Anybody want any more? I got more on the stove."

"No, you eat 'em, Ma," I told her as I got up. "We've all had plenty." I picked up the bag she packed my lunch in, and then looked at Johnny. "I've got to go or I'll be late." He got up, and I said, "Bye, Ma 'n Pa," and went outside. Johnny came out behind me.

"You shouldn't of made those cracks about George Hite in front of Pa an' Ma."

"It's the truth, ain't it?"

"Yeah, I guess, but I need him. No use given' Ma somethin' to fret about."

"It won't bother Pa if he don't have to work. I guess I don't make enough." I was feeling kind of bitter.

"You've been doin' all right, kid," he said, hitting me on the back. "Its just that we've got a good thing there." I felt better as we walked down to the barn, while Johnny talked about how he was going to have rows of junk cars up and down the old pasture and a store room and shop in the barn. It would all cost money, I thought, and he had to borrow my seventeen dollars, but then I thought what the hell? He's my brother.

After we got in the truck and I drove it out of the barn and down the lane, he offered me a cigarette. I shook my head.

"No, thanks. I promised Ma I wouldn't."

"So did I," he said as he put one in his mouth. "A long time ago, but I forgot. I guess she did, too."

I had plenty of time, really. As long as I was in the box factory by seven or a few minutes after, nobody said anything, and it was kind of nice, driving along with the windows open and the smell of spring in the air. Finally Johnny threw his cigarette out the window and settled back, with his hands clasped behind his head.

"Yeah, I've got it all figured out. An' I think it's goin' to work."

"I hope so, Johnny."

He looked at me. "I think you mean that, kid."

I do," I said, looking straight ahead.

"I did learn somethin' in the army. A lot of guys don't. But I did. You got to look out for yourself. Nobody's goin' to do it for you. That's always been the trouble with us Lusts. We been content with other people's leavin'. But I'm goin' to change all that. I'm goin' to get what we've got comin' to us."

"Sellin' junk parts?"

"Yes, by God, sellin' junk parts. In six months I'll be rollin' in dough, enough to set us all up. That's why I got to have George Hite."

"You ain't goin' to get into trouble with him? You know what people say."

"Don't worry about that. There's nothin' to get into that I can't take care of. The army makes boys tough, too, if they let it."

I didn't like the way he sounded, and I wanted to change the subject. "You always was pretty tough. Remember when you licked the Benton kid?"

"He was peanuts compared to what I was up against in the army. No, you don't have to worry about me, kid."

It made me kind of mad to be called kid, but I let it slide like I always do, and Johnny was quiet for a few minutes. Then he began to talk again, almost as if I wasn't there.

"No, I learned a lot of things, all the army wanted to teach me an' more. You got to go out and get what you want. An' you can't worry about steppin' on anybody else's toes. Just make sure nobody steps on yours."

"You can get into trouble talkin' that way."

"Not if you know what you're doin'. An' you got to think ahead, keep a jump ahead of everybody else."

"You're goin' to hurt Ma again, Johnny."

"She's got to learn sometime. Look where this *Do unto others* Christian crap has got her, a doormat and a mattress for an old man for thirty years."

"She's happy when she's doin' for others." He was making me mad again, but I didn't want no argument.

"Happy, hell. Happiness is more than a warm place to sleep and a full belly and a chance to climb onto somethin' every now and then. Hell, dogs have that. Happiness is when you got the dough an' the power to make people jump when you snap your fingers."

"You better shut up, Johnny." I didn't like the look in his eyes, but I couldn't keep still any longer. He just laughed at me. It wasn't a nasty laugh, but I didn't like it.

"Okay, sucker. Have it your way." He laughed again and looked out the window. I was so nervous I almost missed my turn as we came into town, and I been driving it ever since I bought the truck and got my C ration book. Neither of us said anymore until I stopped in front of the factory gate. Johnny chuckled as I got out and he slid over under the wheel. I didn't look at him. "Want me to pick you up at four?"

"You'd better. I don't want to walk home."

"Okay, kid." He put the truck in gear and started up as I turned to go in the gate and punch my card.

There were three or four guys hanging around the clock station when I went to get my card. I'd seen them around, so I nodded. As I pulled my card out of the rack, I noticed a paper clipped to it, but I didn't pay any attention. I just remembered that I left my lunch in the truck, and I only had twenty or thirty cents in my pocket. Maybe Johnny would notice and bring it back, I thought, as I put the card in the slot on the clock.

"You got one, too, huh, kid?" somebody said behind me.

"Got one what?" I said as I pushed the lever on the clock.

"Layoff slip. There, on your card." The other men behind him laughed as I looked at it.

"I was thinkin' of somethin' else," I mumbled. I didn't know what else to say.

"You better think about kissing that stitching machine goodbye. The war's over, kid." The man turned away as I read the slip.

It didn't say much, just that due to cancelled contracts, I was laid off, that today was my last day, that I was eligible for unemployment compensation. It made me feel pretty lousy. I wished Johnny would come back with the truck. I'd say the hell with them now and go work in the junkyard. Instead, I went inside and the boss put me to work loading what he said was the last shipment. The way he said it made me mad at first, but he couldn't help it. The war was over and maybe nobody needed any boxes anymore. I worked pretty steady, piling knock down boxes in a big truck, and the morning went pretty fast. Pretty soon I quit thinking about it. I just wished I hadn't forgot my lunch.

I went out at noon to get a sandwich, and Johnny was waiting outside the gate with the truck. As I went over, I saw that George Hite was with him. I didn't like for him to be in my truck. He was just no good and people would talk, sceing Johnny with him, but what could I do about it?

"Thought you might be gettin' a little hungry." Johnny held up the bag, and I took it through the window.

"You can have one of the sandwiches," I told him.

"We ate up town," Hite put in. I made like I didn't hear him.

"Ma always puts in plenty," I went on.

"You eat it, kid. I ate."

"Thanks for bringin' it, Johnny."

"Had to, didn't I?" Johnny grinned. "I didn't want to lug home a corpse tonight. Growin' boy needs his food, don't he?"

I laughed. "No danger. I'm pretty healthy."

George Hite leaned forward then, with a nasty grin. "They give you the axe, too, huh?"

"What do you know about it?"

"I hear things. I know what's goin' on around this town."

Johnny looked at me. "Did they, Bobby?"

"Yeah." I opened the bag and looked inside. There were three sandwiches made out of leftover chicken.

"The offer's still open. The hell with 'em."

I looked at George Hite and then back at Johnny. "Guess it looks like I'll have to. I got to do somethin'."

George Hite laughed. "Hell, you sound like it's a funeral. Nobody's got a gun in your back."

Johnny looked at him quickly. "Shut up. Let the kid make up his own mind."

"When you want me to start?" I asked Johnny.

"Whenever you're ready, kid."

I turned to go back in. "See you tonight," I said. I felt a little better, Johnny was boss, at least. I wouldn't work for George Hite.

"Yeah." Johnny started the motor. I didn't look back at them. I was thinking about what I'd do if the guys loafed all afternoon like they said. I wanted a good record, at least, even if I was laid off.

Chapter 4

All the time I was eating my lunch I felt kind of low. It wasn't much fun getting laid off from a job. For some reason I never figured I would, as long as I did my work as good as I could and wasn't absent or late or didn't horse around like some of the other fellows, but the war was over and that was that. I supposed I should be glad because now that it was over, all the boys would be coming home, and I wouldn't have to feel so bad about Pa making me stay home from the war to help him and Ma. At least I wouldn't have to talk to the guys at work about it any more, or have somebody ask me about why I wasn't in the army.

There was lots of good things going to happen, too, now that the war was over. Things wouldn't be so hard to get, for one thing, and all the ads in the magazines said everything was going to be so much better. It was a little hard to swallow, especially when the pictures would show a soldier in a foxhole thinking of a new car or a refrigerator, and it was even harder to take now that the box factory was closed. There wasn't anything else to do in Titus for a job. I was kind of glad when the whistle blew to go back to work.

I did my work the best I could, all afternoon, though, even if some of the guys did go around chalking up dirty sayings about the bosses and especially about the guy who owned the factory, Mr. Harris. Besides, I wasn't used to loading trucks, and I got pretty tired. I was sure glad when we got the last one loaded. It was only two-thirty, and the boss told us to sit around until quitting time at three-thirty, or else go home, whichever we wanted. I had to wait for Johnny anyway, so I went out back and sat down. It was sure nice, sitting in the sun, and I almost forgot about getting laid off.

Pretty soon one of the guys from the factory came out and sat down beside me. I'd seen him around a lot, so I said, "Hi." He was a lot older tham me, and I didn't know what else to say. He lit up a cigarette and then leaned back against the building.

"Pretty soft, hey son, sittin' around, gettin' paid for it."

"I guess so. I guess I'd rather gone home though."

"You can go. They wouldn't mind. Hell, it would save 'em some money. It's a wonder .pa

they didn't chase us all out right away, now there's nothin' to do."

"An extra hour don't mean much to them, I guess. But I got to wait for my brother to pick me up. He's usin' my truck," I added, just to feel important, I guess.

"Pretty young to be havin' a truck of your own, ain't you?"

"I'm eighteen. Old enough. My brother's just home from the army."

"Say, you ain't Joe Lust's boy, are you?"

"Yeah. That's Pa." I picked up a piece of stick and started to break it with my fingers.

"You're the youngest one, then. I used to know your Pa. Come to think of it, I saw your brother down to the pool room last night. Maybe the judge thought the army'd kinda tame him a bit when he made him go, but he was sure talkin' pretty big last night. Got lots more gumption than your old man ever had." The man shook his head and kind of laughed. It made me mad. What the hell business was it of his? I'd almost forgotten about the judge making Johnny go to the army and Ma getting sick over it and having to take pills to put her to sleep. Why couldn't people leave us alone?

I threw a stick down on the ground and got up. "I guess I'll go wait in front. He might be a little early."

"You got lots of time. Did your Pa ever tell you about when he worked for Mason, the contractor, last summer? Old man Mason couldn't get any men, so he..."

Whatever the man said, I didn't hear anymore. I didn't want to. I almost ran back into the building. I knew what he'd say anyway, what everybody said. It was no secret, everybody in town said the same, but I didn't have to listen any more. It wasn't like when I was a kid. Now I was big enough so I didn't have to listen. Nobody could make me.

I walked through the factory to the front. Nobody was around, and I was glad of that. I didn't want to see anybody, not even Johnny with the truck right then. I walked on through and punched my card. Let them have the extra hour, I figured. As long as I didn't have to listen to people laugh. I went out and sat on the curb.

I remembered a lot of things, sitting there on the curb. I remembered a town kid not wanting to sit with me in school, and I didn't know why. I remembered them laugh when I tripped and dropped a fly playing ball at recess. I remembered the kids nudge each other and look when a man gave me an old rusty pair of skates and I took them to school. Other kids took things to school. Most of all I remembered what they did to Ma.

Ma went to a different church then, a big, red-brick one in town, with carpets on the floor, and colored windows that made you look pale when the sun shone through. It was a big church, and a nice one, and I used to go, with Ma, even if Johnny and Pa didn't. I went to Sunday School, too, but I didn't like that. It was mostly the same kids from school. But I liked the service and the church and the music and the minister's soft, easy voice. Sometimes I even kind of hated it to be over.

Then one Sunday we were late. Pa's old car wouldn't start at first, but Ma made him fix it. I was just as glad; I wouldn't have to go to Sunday School. Then, finally we got started, and when Pa let us out, I could hear singing inside. I didn't want to go in. People always looked when you were late. But Ma said to come on, and we went up the steps and into the church.

It was a warm Sunday in Spring, and the doors were wide open. The church was crowded, too, more so than usual, so we stood there for a minute, waiting for one of the men to find us a seat. But none of them came, they were busy, I guess. Finally I saw some room in a seat about halfway down the aisle. I pointed it out to Ma.

"Look, Ma, there's a seat. Room enough for you."

"Where? I don't see it, son." Ma spoke kind of loud.

"There." I pointed again. A man in the back row turned around and looked, and so did a woman, but I didn't pay any attention. "Behind the lady in the yellow hat. You can make 'em move in. There's plenty of room in the seat."

I must of talked louder than I thought, because other people turned around, too, but Ma started down the aisle.

One thing about Ma then, she certainly walked straight. She wasn't so heavy then, either, and she walked kind of easy. People loked like they always did when you were late, but Ma didn't even notice. She stopped where I showed her and looked down at the person at the end of the seat. It was a little girl, one I used to see sometimes in school. Ma half- turned and motioned to the girl and started to step into the row. Then she stepped back, but I couldn't see why. I stepped out in the aisle as Ma motioned to the girl again, and without looking at Ma, the girl shook her head quick. Ma turned away then, slow, and looked around, her hands still out in front, kind of like she was still motioning someone to let her in. It seemed like an hour, but she stood there, alone in the middle of the long purple carpet, and nobody moved except Ma.

I wanted to run down the aisle and make the girl let Ma sit down, or yell not to make her stand there, or find her a seat. But I didn't. I just stood there watching. Finally Ma tuned to come back toward me. The music stopped then, and the minister stood up to talk. Everyone looked at him, their heads all up straight. Nobody looked at Ma.

We stood in the back for the rest of the service, till finally, when it was almost over, one of the men from the church brought Ma a chair. I felt like telling him what he could do, but Ma sat down just like nothing had happened. All during the service I didn't hear the minister, didn't hear the music, or anything. I just kept thinking what I'd like to do to all of them, especially to the little girl, all the mean things I could think of. But Ma listened and prayed and when it was over, she folded up the chair so people could pass.

Ma went out right at first but I kind of hung back, hoping I would see the little girl, so I could bump her on the steps. Finally she came out with a lady and a man, and I slipped in behind. The lady was saying something, and as I got set to push, I couldn't help hearing.

"You could have moved over. We had pleanty of room."

"But mother, that nasty old woman."

"It wouldn't have hurt. You could've sat close to me."

"But mother, would God want me to let her in?"

The lady said something about God, but I stopped and let them go on. I never thought like that about God before. I guess I never thought much about him at all. The minister talked about him, and I listened, and memorized stuff and listened to the stories, but I never thought about God. Now, all of a sudden, he became real, and he was just like the rest of them. All of a sudden I was scared, and I ran down the steps. Ma was down at the corner, watching for Pa. She kind of half-smiled as I caught up to her.

I never said anything about it to Ma, and never was sure she thought about it, but I quit going to church much after that. It was never the same--the minister and the music and the cool inside light didn't mean much anymore. I remembered the little girl and what she said about God. One day, though, at school, I bumped her real hard, but even that didn't make me feel better. She went and told the teacher, and I had to tell her I was sorry. The teacher said I was a rude little boy.

It wasn't long after that they started a new church, and Ma began to go there. It was in an old store building painted white, and the benches were hard and the minister talked about a God who was as mean as the little girl's, and the music was a piano and sometimes a horn. I went with Ma once or twice, and then I didn't go anymore. She kept after me for a while, and then she let me alone. I kind of quit thinking about God after that.

The factory whistle blew then all of a sudden, and I kind of jumped as I got up off of the curb. I was tired of sitting, and I started looking for Johnny. The rest of the guys came out of the factory, some of them talking, but most walking along pretty quiet. I wondered where they would find any jobs. Maybe it was a good thing Johnny was starting the junkyard after all. I started to walk down the street, hoping Johnny would come. But after a while guys were gone, and still Johnny hadn't showed up.

I began to feel pretty mean again, thinking what he might be doing with my truck. Now I didn't have a job, it was all I had, and Pa didn't even want me to buy that. I kept thinking about Johnny forgetting to look at the oil, or maybe blowing a tire, or smashing it up. Finally, though, he pulled up at the curb.

"Hey, Bobby. Think I wasn't comin'?" He was grinning like he must of thought it was funny.

"It's about time. I been out of work for an hour." I waited for him to move over, but he didn't, so I walked around and got in.

He shot off, screeching the tires.

"Take it easy, Johnny. What you trin' to do?"

"Hell, kid, no sense in babyin' it like you do."

"It's the only truck I got, ain't it? I got to take care of it."

"When the new ones come out, you can trade it in."

"With what? It took me long enough to pay for this one."

Johnny laughed. "On the dough you were makin' in that place, I can really believe it."

"An' I'm out of a job, remember?"

"You're workin' for me, ain't you, kid?"

"Yeah. I guess. All the more reason to make it last."

Johnny really laughed at that, but I didn't feel any better. The way the motor sounded, we'd be lucky to get home. But he didn't seem to even hear it, just kept laughing and twisting the wheel. Finally he looked at me.

"You're a funny kid, Bobby."

"Why? Just 'cause I want to take care of my truck?"

"You take things too Goddamn seriously all the time."

"Somebody's got to. You sure don't seem to care."

"Kid, you got so much to learn it ain't even funy."

"Like the junk business, for instance?"

"Maybe. But it ain't only that. There's plenty of angles if you only use your head. You stick with me, kid, an' you won't worry about an old truck or a lousy job or anythin' else. You'll be able to get whatever you want, a car, a woman, or anythin' else."

Johnny slapped his hand on the wheel. "Keerist! Do I have to draw you a picture?"

"Maybe so. I guess I'm just pretty dumb."

"Sure the new models ain't out yet. An' the longer they take, the better off we're gonna be. That's the beauty of a junkyard. People got to have parts. Then when they do come out, you'll have the dough to buy what you want."

I didn't say anything because we were almost home. As we came up the hill, I could see Stella standing in the yard. Johnny must of seen her too, because he blew the horn as we pulled into the lane.

"There's a woman, Bobby. You can get one of those, too, if you study the angles. Then you'll have something worth frettin' about."

"Sure," I said, and got out as soon as he stopped. I went in the house without even saying "Hi" to Stella. I felt pretty low. I was out of a job and in the junk business, and it still didn't make sense.

Chapter 5

Johnny didn't seem to be in any hurry for me to start working, though, so I didn't do much the next four or five days, just hung around the house and the barn and fiddled around with my truck whenever Johnny hadn't borrowed it. He was off in it a lot, though, getting things set up, he said. He brought home a couple of loads of stuff--tools and lumber and a second-hand paint spray outfit--and I helped him and George Hite unload. They didn't say where they got the stuff and I didn't ask. But it must of cost money.

I kind of wanted to talk to somebody to see what they thought about me workin' for Johnny, but I didn't know who. I knew how Pa felt, and Ma probably felt like Pa did, but still I wasn't sure how it would work out. I remembered when Johnny bossed me sometimes before, and I didn't go for it much. Still, it ought to work out all right, I figured. We were older now and ought to have good sense and not fight like a couple of kids. If only George Hite wasn't in it.

It was hard getting used to sleeping in the kitchen, especially with Johnny and Stella in my room right off it talking and all, but I got used to it. It was easier to get up, too, but it was kind of hard to dress 'cause Ma was usually fixing breakfast and then Pa'd come in and then Johnny. Stella slept pretty late. I was glad of that. I didn't like her knowing about me sleeping in the kitchen as it was.

Stella wasn't much good around the house, though, and it kind of got me. Whatever got done, Ma did, like always, and Stella was in the bedroom or reading in some books she had or looking for Johnny. I tried to shame her by helping once in a while, but it didn't do any good. Johnny didn't say anything about it to her, and she'd wipe dishes once in a while but that was all. The hard stuff, like washing clothes, Ma did herself. She'd look at Stella, once in a while, but she didn't say anything either.

When Johnny brought out all his army stuff, Ma had a big wash, but Stella didn't make no move to help, so I did. Ma didn't say anything to me, but I could tell she was kind of pleased, even though she did talk about me going back to Sunday School. I didn't even like to think about it, and I hadn't for a long time. It would be all right, I guess, if people were like the Bible and the preacher and Ma said, but I knew better. I hate to have people look at me and make funny cracks, so I just never went back anymore. Ma was the only one went to church, in the little new one in town. I'd drive her in and pick her up, but I didn't go in anymore. She liked it, and I guess she didn't mind the preacher and the music and the God they talked about, or else she didn't care.

All the time I was helping her wring the clothes, I kept thinking this, and she must of figured I wasn't paying any attention, so after a while she quit talking about it. I wanted to talk to her about something, though, so when we were out in the yard hanging up clothes, I asked her what she thought about Johnny's junkyard business. She didn't say anything until she finished hanging up one of Johnny's jackets and then she turned to look at me, holding up her hand to shade her eyes from the sun. It was pretty bright.

39

"You Pa thinks it's a pretty good idea, son. Maybe if I hadn't of laughed at some of his ideas, things'd be different now."

"I know," I said. "But that ain't the point."

"A junkyard is an honest business. An' Johnny needs somethin' to do that'll provide for him and her."

"You think it's all right then."

"I guess."

"Johnny gets some pretty big ideas sometimes."

"I know." She turned to hang up a shirt while I stood there. I knew there was more on her mind, but Ma kept a lot of things to herself. It made it hard to talk to her most of the time.

"I guess I'm goin' to work for him, Ma," I said.

"You got to remember you're brothers." She had a clothes pin in her mouth and it was hard to understand her.

"Is it a good idea or ain't it, Ma?"

She turned around to face me then and took the clothes pin out of her mouth. "It ain't like workin' for somebody else, you know. But I tried to do the best I could for you boys. Maybe not good enough, I don't know, but the best I know how. It ain't been easy with your Pa like he is. I hope it'll be all right, son. Just try to get along. It's hard sometimes, but that's what you got to do."

"I'll do my best, Ma."

"An' look out for Johnny, son. He needs lookin' after."

Johnny came around the house then, and I was glad I didn't have to answer. I knew how Ma felt about

Johnny. But I guess he gave Ma more to think about than I did.

"Anybody takin' my name in vain?" He laughed like he was in a good mood, and then looked at the stuff on the line. "I used to have to send all this stuff to the G.I. laundry," he said. "I'm sure glad those days are over."

Ma kind of laughed, like she was glad about it too, and didn't say anything. I just wished he didn't make Ma do all the work while Stella was reading her books.

Johnny looked at me then. "You had enough vacation yet, kid?"

"Sure," I said. I looked at Ma, but she kept watching Johnny.

"It's about time we did somethin' about the barn then."

"What you want done to it?" I asked him. I was kind of anxious to have something to do. It keeps you from fretting.

"It's easier to show you than to tell," he said. "Come on down an' I'll show you."

I looked at Ma again, but she was picking up another shirt, so I followed Johnny down to the barn. He showed me what to haul out and where he wanted space to work on cars, and I listened, not saying much. I could get along if I put my mind to it, and I was going to .pa

try. I wished he'd stop calling me kid, though, but he didn't, and I let it go. It wasn't worth fussing about.

After a while we went up to the house. Ma'd gone back in and we stood by the door.

"Pa says he's goin' to help," Johnny said after a while. "I don't know how much good he'll be, but try to keep him happy. I told him it was okay," he added. "He'll get sick of it after a while."

"I suppose. He's got a bad back."

"Yeah." Johnny laughed and then looked down the road. "Okay if we use the truck for a while?" he asked.

"Sure, Johnny," I said. "The keys are in it." I went in the house then. What the hell, I figured. It wasn't much to ask.

Chapter 6

It was good having something to do again for a
change, even if it was working in the old barn, and I
puttered around, carting out junk and raking up hay till
Ma called me to come up to the house and have something to eat. Johnny didn't come home, and it was just
Pa and Ma and Stella and me. It was a pretty good dinner, though, liver and fried potatoes, and I was pretty
hungry. I ate in a hurry without saying much and got
up to go. As I swallowed the last bite, Stella got up,
too. She didn't eat as much or as fast as I always did.
She followed me out the side door. She had something
in her hand.

"Bobby, wait. I want to ask you to do me a favor."

I stopped by the well, wondering what she wanted.
She could of asked Johnny. She knew I was working in
the barn now, while Johnny was going and coming all
the time.

"I suppose I got time. What do you want, Stella?"

She kind of looked around quickly. I don't know
why. There was nobody except Pa and Ma in the
kitchen, and they couldn't hear anyway. I kind of
wished I didn't say okay, though.

"I'll walk on down toward the barn with you and tell
you on the way. I can use some air, anyway. I've been
spending too much time in the house these days." She
laughed a little as we walked along, but it sounded
kind of nervous. She sure looked good, though, in
black slacks and a black sweater, and I didn't mind too

much, really. It was kind of nice having her around. I could just see over the top of her head. I always liked girls that tall. We didn't say anything until down by the barn when we scared a rabbit out of some high weeds. It was a young one, and it ran down the lane for a ways in front of us. Stella laughed again, kind of excited this time, and she grabbed my arm. We stopped to watch it run under the barn.

"Oh, I never saw a wild rabbit that close before, Bobby."

"There's lots of 'em around here," I said offhand, but I felt kind of excited too as she held onto my arm. I never thought it could be something to watch young rabbits run before. "I'll take you out in the woods one of these days. There's lots of 'em out there. Once in a while you can see a skunk or woodchuck, or even a deer, sometimes."

She wrinkled up her nose at that. "Ooh, a skunk, Bobby?"

"They're kind of pretty," I said, "if you don't get too close."

"I wouldn't want to get close enough to find out whether they're pretty or not," she said. Then, like she just remembered she was still holding my arm, she let go. After a minute we started to walk down toward the barn again. I felt like asking her if she wanted to go out in the woods then, but I didn't. I had work to do, and probably Johnny wouldn't like it. Still, it would be fun showing her things. I'd forgot she was a city girl from Boston and didn't know much about things like that.

When we got to the barn, we stopped in front of the door for a minute. "It's pretty messy inside," I told her. "You'd probably get your feet dirty." She was just wearing little sandals.

"It's all right. I don't mind a little dirt."

"We've got an old bench inside. I can drag it out here in the shade."

"You don't have to. I'll have to be getting back to the house."

"Why?" I asked without thinking. She kind of blushed, and I looked away. It was one of those things you just come out and ask.

"I guess I'm not much good around here, am I Bobby?"

"I didn't mean that." I was kind of embarrassed. "Wait a minute and' I'll drag that bench out here." I almost ran in the barn. When I pulled it out a couple of minutes later, she was standing there with her arms folded across her chest. I saw what she had in her hand. It was a letter. I wondered if she wanted me to mail it, if that was the favor. If so, she should of asked Johnny. Otherwise things didn't look right. She smiled, though, as I pulled the bench up against the side of the barn.

"It's so quiet out here, Bobby. Almost as though we're the only people in the world. No one but us and the birds," she added after a second as a bird flew by almost touching us.

"It is pretty quiet," I said. "I never thought much about it before."

"But I like it. Right now it's just what I was expecting. Quiet, peaceful, no one around." She sat down on the bench. "This is the way I always wanted to live. Just like it is this moment." She leaned back on the bench, up against the side of the barn. I just stood there looking at her, not knowing what I should say. I wasn't sure she was even talking to me. It was more like she was thinking out loud. But she looked up at me and smiled again. She sure was a pretty girl when she smiled.

"Why don't you sit down and enjoy it, Bobby? You don't have to start working again right away, do you?"

"I should, I suppose," I said, but I sat down anyway. It sure was nice and quiet and warm, and the sky was blue, full of fluffy white clouds. I never noticed that kind of thing much before, but it really was nice. Still, I was kind of worried about the letter. If she asked me, I wasn't sure whether I'd mail it or not.

"I suppose you sure miss Boston an' all your friends an' everthin'," I said just to have something to say.

She didn't answer right away, but just kept looking out at the sky and the line of woods on the far side of Bill Glen's wheat field. Then she looked at me. "No, Bobby, I don't. It may sound a little funny to you that I don't, but I haven't even thought about them much. Until last night, that is, when Johnny was out and I didn't have anything else to do. But when Johnny's around, I never miss any of it."

"But there's so much more to do an' see in the city, and so much more goin' on all the time. I think I'd like it."

"No, you wouldn't, Bobby. Not the way you have to live if you don't have anything. Then you're on the outside looking in. It's not very pleasant unless you're good at kidding yourself."

I thought about that a minute. I had a pretty good idea of what she was talking aobut. I felt the same way too many times, right around here. "If that's the way it is, there ain't a whole lot of difference from here. An' people don't know you, at least," I said without looking at her.

"Sometimes that's the worst part about it. People don't know you, don't even know or care if you're alive."

"I don't see how that could be worse than havin' people stare at you or laugh or make fun of you. That's pretty bad, too. But in a city, if it's big enough, that doesn't happen." I wanted to change the subject all of a sudden, but Stella didn't give me a chance.

"They stare, too, sometimes at you and sometimes right through you, and if you have to live where I did, there's plenty of people to laugh and make fun and think you're fair game for anyone who wants to catch you in a doorway or a crowded subway and put his hands on you."

I really wanted to change the subject then. "At least you got inside plumbing in a city. An' parks an' things like that."

"Sure we've got all that. We had inside plumbing in the place I was raised. On the top floor of a four-story walkup. And four families sharing the same bathroom, if I can call it that. And half the time the water pressure was so low that it didn't get up that far. It's not all that bad, but it was the best I knew, and I couldn't take any more. The noise of water pounding in the pipes,

and squalling kids at the door if you were in too long."
She looked down at her feet. "We had parks, too, lots
of them. There's no place like the Common and the
Public Garden in the spring, and you can lie on the
grass and watch the swan boats on the pond or stare at
the sky or watch a ball game. And then somebody
steps on you or kicks sand in your face or tries to pick
you up, thinking that's all you're waiting around for."

I never thought it could be like that in the city. I
never thought about it before, and I didn't want to
now, so I got up. "I got to go back to work now, Stella.
We've got an awful lot of stuff to do in the barn."

"You're a funny kid, Bobby. What's eating you all
the time? What are you afraid of?"

"I ain't afraid of anythin'. There's just no use frettin'
about things, that's all. There's nothin' you can do
about it anyway, so frettin' don't help."

"Do you really believe that, Bobby? That there's
nothing you can do about things except put up with
them?"

"Why now?" All of a sudden I felt like there were a
lot of things I wanted to get off my chest too. "I never
saw anybody able to do anything about things. An' I
never saw prayin' do any good. Ma does plenty of it,
an' it hasn't done any good that I know of."

"I used to think that way too, Bobby, pretty much
the same way, anyhow, especially after I graduated and
went to work in that restaurant. I wasn't much of a
place, but a lot of service men ate there. You had to
take a lot, and ten hours a day on your feet is pretty
bad, but the tips were good. I hated it, hated the things

you have to do for money. And then Johnny came in one day."

"An' that made a difference, huh? He was someone who could change things for you?"

"I guess that's the way I felt. Anyway, it made all the difference in the world. I wasn't the best girl in the world, maybe because I felt what's the use, too. And then he made me feel like somebody. I just liked to hear him talk. I felt that if anyone could change things, Johnny could."

"Johnny always could talk, all right. An' change things," I said, but she didn't even act like she heard me.

"How could I miss all that? How could I ever want it back? And when Johnny talked about the farm, and how he was going into business, I knew that's what I wanted, too." She was quiet for a minute, and I just stood there, not saying anything either. I didn't want to go to work anymore. I just wanted to listen to her. It sure was quiet, just standin' there without talking. I seemed like I almost knew what Stella was thinking.

I heard a motor then and turned around. My truck was pulling into the lane. Johnny must of seen us, or me anyway, because he tooted the horn. I waved, and he slowed up and stopped by the house. As he got out of the truck, Stella jumped up.

"Bobby, there's something I want you to do. When you go into town, will you mail this letter for me?" She held it out. "I don't have any stamps."

"That's okay," I said, taking it. "I can get some at the post office." I glanced down at it. It was addressed to a girl, and I figured it was all right.

She started to turn away, and then stopped. "One other thing, Bobby. Don't tell Johnny about it. He probably wouldn't understand why I wanted to write." She turned then and started up the lane toward the house. I watched her a minute, thinking how pretty she was, and how nice when you got to know her. I went in the barn then, and put the letter down on my boxes in the corner. I put some straw over it, figuring I could get it when I got a chance to go into town. Then I started to work, raking stuff up in a pile so I could haul it out and burn it when I got it all together. I must of worked for a half an hour or so, piling stuff up and trying to figure out where I could borrow a wheel barrow. It was pretty warm, and I never liked raking much, but I felt kind of good, and I felt sorry for Stella. I figured I'd be as nice as I could to her from then on.

Johnny came in then, while I was standing around, trying to cool off. He looked at me and grinned.

"My God, this place stinks." He looked around. "This stuff must of been layin' around for fifteen years."

"At least, I guess." I wiped off some of the sweat.

"You don't have to kill yourself, kid. Don't do it all at once."

"I won't, I said, and started to rake again. Johnny started looking around the barn. I remembered the letter all of a sudden but there was nothing I could do then. I just hoped he wouldn't notice the boxes, but I was afraid that he would. I wished I'd put the letter inside.

"You know anyplace we can borrow a wheel barrow, Johnny?" I asked, hoping he'd quit looking around.

"George an' me'll try to pick up a second-hand one tomorrow," he said. "We're goin' to need one, anyway."

"Yeah." I kept on raking and he kept on looking around.

Johnny kicked something over in the corner then. As soon as I heard it, I knew it was my boxes.

"Bobby, what's this stuff over here in the corner?"

"Just some junk I been savin'. I'll get it out of here."

"No, you don't have to do that. We got plenty of room. You might even fix yourself up a corner. I know how you like to save things, kid. You might as well. Keeps you out of poolrooms." He laughed and then said, "Hey, there's a letter over here under the hay."

"It's mine. I put it there." I kept on raking. I was afraid to look to see if he was picking it up.

"It's Stella's handwriting. Addressed to that God-damn slut she used to run with in Boston." He came over to me with it in his hand. "What's it doin' out here? She give it to you to mail?"

I nodded. "So what? She can write to her friends."

"No." He tore the letter in two while I watched him. There was nothing I could do to stop him.

"Listen, kid, there's one thing I want you to get straight right now. She wanted to get out of there, okay, I got her out. On my terms, an' she knows it." He tore the letter up into little bits and dropped them on the heap of trash. "She's not to have anythin' to do with anybody unless I say so. Remember that. I'm not standin' for anythin' goin' on behind my back. If she asks you to do somethin' like this again, you tell her no. Understand?"

"She's got a right to have friends."

"Not unless I say so, hear? She's mine. Every God-damn bit of her. An' I ain't sharin' with nobody, no matter who."

"What am I supposed to say if she asks me about the letter?"

"She won't have to. I'll tell her."

"Okay. If that's the way you want it." I felt pretty mad, but what could I do?

"That's the way it is, kid." He turned then toward the door. "You just tend to your own affairs out here. I'll take care of Stella. That's what I married her for."

He went out without looking back. It was funny almost. He didn't sound mad, just cold, like he really didn't care about her any more than he would about a good prize dog. I sure felt sorry for Stella right then. I kept on raking for a while and then went outside and sat on the bench, but it didn't seem as nice as before, sitting there by myself. After a while I went up to the house and swept out the cab of my truck. It was full of cigarette butts, and it made me kind of mad.

Chapter 7

Stella didn't say anything about the letter for a few days, and I figured that Johnny'd told her he tore it up. I just hoped that she wouldn't ask me to do anything like that again. It wasn't anything, mailing a letter, but I just didn't want to get mixed up in it. Johnny could get pretty mean when he wanted to, and where Stella was concerned, I figured he would want to. The less you mix into things, the better off you are, anyway.

Everything went on pretty much the same, Johnny coming and going all the time, mostly with George Hite, and me working in the barn. Pa came in sometimes ahd helped, but most of the time he would stand around and boss me for a while. I didn't pay much attention though, even if he did say that when the real work that took brains started, he was really going to pitch in and do things. I hoped he wouldn't though. He'd just get in the way. But you couldn't tell him that.

Stella hung around the house, not saying much, just waiting for Johnny, and when she was expecting him getting herself all fixed up. Most of the time, though, there was no telling

when to expect him. It sure wasn't much like him having a regular job. I wouldn't go for it myself, at all, chasing around like that.

Then, a couple of days later, when I was out washing up at the pump just before supper, Stella came out and sat down on the well stone. She was wearing her slacks and had her hair all fixed nice for Johnny. She talked to me kind of generally while I washed, and I was thinking she ought to be in the house helping Ma fix supper. Still, it was nice friendly talk like you can't do with a girl very often. Then, as I was wiping my face, she put one leg up on the stone and clasped her hands around it. She looked at me, and I mumbled something about sure being hungry.

She smiled at that and then asked, "Bobby, did you get a chance to get into town and mail my letter yet?"

I started to rub my face real hard with the towel, and she didn't say anymore for a minute. Then as I put the towel down, she asked, "Did you?"

I hung the towel up real careful on the hook.

"You don't have to be afraid to tell me you forgot." She laughed like girls do. "Did you forget, Bobby?"

I didn't know what to say. I didn't want to tell her about it if Johnny didn't. and I didn't want to lie for him, either.

She laughed again. "You forgot, didn't you, Bobby?"

I figured what the hell. "No, Stella, I didn't forget. I didn't mail it, either."

"I know it's not easy to do things with Johnny using your truck all the time. But it doesn't really matter, Bobby. You don't have to be so serious about it. It isn't that important. It was just to my girlfriend. I wanted to tell her how quiet and easy it was here and make her a little bit jealous. There's no hurry." She spoke kind of fast, like she thought she was making things easier for me.

Her talking like that just made me feel worse. I wished she'd quit talking about it, but she went on. She really didn't get much chance to say anything to anybody around the house, I guess, and there sure wasn't much to talk about anyway.

"The only reason I asked you was because Johnny just doesn't understand. And if he knew that I was bragging a little, he really would laugh." She got a little serious then. "He says that part of my life is over, and I'm not even supposed to look back. He wants his wife to be a lady, not a hash-slinger, I guess." She jumped up suddenly then and turned to me, with her hands on her hips. She looked kind of mad. "Bobby, you didn't tell Johnny about the letter, did you?"

"He found it where I hid it in the barn. I didn't tell him," I said, looking away. "He found it himself, where I put it away."

"What did he do with it? He didn't mail it, I know. He wouldn't. He told me I was through with all of them. I know he wouldn't mail it."

"He said he was goin' to tell you. He tore it up."

"He tore it up," she said real low. "He had no right. It was none of his business. He said I was through with all that and I agreed because I wanted to get away, but still he had no right, and I'm going to tell him so. I've got a life of my own, even if he doesn't think so, and I'm not his property or any one else's." She sounded pretty mad.

I didn't know what to say to her, so I just stared down the lane, wishing that Johnny wouldn't of seen the letter. It would of been so much easier that way, but things never seem to work out the easy way. I didn't blame Stella for getting mad, though. Johnny sure liked to run everything. But there wasn't much you could do about it most of the time. Johnny wouldn't let you.

Stella didn't say any more then, but went in the house. I stood aorund outside for a while, thinking how quiet it was, just like Stella said, with no noise except the crickets and the birds and once in a while a car barrelling down the highway. Finally though, I figured I might as well go in. If we hurried up and ate, and Johnny didn't come home until late, Stella would probably forget about it. I didn't like to think about how mad he'd be if she said anything. Still, I wouldn't see why he couldn't of told her like he said he was going to do instead of letting her find out this way. It all seemed so sneaky, kind of.

I sure was glad when supper was over and Johnny didn't come in, even if Stella did do quite a bit of talking all the time we ate. She laughed a lot, too, mostly when there didn't seem to be much of anything to laugh at. She seemed kind of nervous, though, and she spilled half a bowl of gravy, but she even laughed at that. Pa did too, but Ma didn't think it was so funny. Ma never went much for laughing, though.

After supper Ma and Stella did the dishes, and Stella even tried to joke with Ma a little, but she didn't get very far, and they finished without talking at all, like they usually did. Pa yawned a little for a while and then went to bed. I hung around the kitchen, hoping to get a chance to tell Stella not to tell Johnny, but after they finished the dishes, she went in the bedroom. She left the door open, though, and I could see her laying on the bed reading. She didn't seem to be turning any pages, though, like she really wasn't reading, but I couldn't tell for sure.

As soon as Ma went to bed, I figured, I'd go in and tell Stella not to say anything about it. It wouldn't change things any, and Johnny'd just get mad. But instead of going in the front room, where her and Pa slept, she started to set up her ironing board. I watched her for a minute and then when she got the legs tangled or something, I got up to help.

"You shouldn't have to iron tonight, Ma," I said.

"It's got to get done, Bobby. An' it's my job. Besides, it doesn't heat up the house so in the evenin'."

I got the legs straightened out then, and got it set up. It was pretty rickety, though. It was probably older than me.

"Looks like this board is on its last legs, Ma," I said, trying to be funny. "You sure need a new one."

"Lots of things we need new, son. But they really ain't important. As long as they do the things they're supposed to."

"Someday, Ma, if things go all right, you ain't goin' to have to put up with a lot of old junk. You'll be able to get new whenever you want." For the first time all of a sudden I felt pretty good about the junkyard business. What Johnny said was true, parts were really hard to get, and the new models everybody was talking about still looked like a long way off. As soon as we really got started, we'd be able to get Ma things like a new ironing board.

Ma got a basket of clothes then and started to damp them. I figured I wasn't going to get a chance to talk to Stella then, so I pulled up a chair and watched Ma. It sure looked easy, like everything she did, but after a few minutes there was drops of water on her face and her hair started to fall down in front.

"Ma, you ought to quit for a while. Or even get Stella to help some. She probably would if you asked."

"I ain't askin' her to do anythin'. She knows what's got to be done. If she wants to help, all right. But it's my job, an' I'll do it." She kind of smiled as she pushed her hair up out of her eyes. "It's really not so bad, an' it's got to be done. Besides, I like to work." She turned away and picked up her iron to see if it was hot. "Workin's better than broodin'. Work keeps you from thinkin'."

She said it so low I could hardly hear, but I knew what she meant. That's what happened to Pa. It never would happen to Ma, though. She wouldn't let it. She'd work till she couldn't do anymore, and then she'd go to bed. But sometimes she'd cry out in her sleep.

Ma kept ironing, mostly Johnny's stuff, but a lot of Stella's and mine and Pa's. There wasn't much of her own. it didn't seem fair, even if that was the way it was. But Ma never was one to complain. After a while I got tired of sitting there, so I went over to the couch and picked up a magazine that was laying there. I figured if Ma didn't go to bed pretty soon, I wouldn't get a chance to say anything to Stella.

I got started reading a story, though, and kind of forgot. It was an interesting story about a man who was mistaken for somebody else, but it was hard to follow and didn't make too much sense. I finished it and sat there trying to figure it out when I heard the truck pull up into the yard. And Ma was still ironing.

Johnny came in after a minute, looking like he was feeling pretty good. He said "Hi", grinning and made a playful swing at me with a newspaper he had. He threw it down on the table then as Ma put down her iron.

"I'll fix you somethin' to eat, Johnny. Sit down and I'll warm up the stew an' make a fresh pot of coffee."

"Never mind, Ma. I got somethin' to eat in town."

"You ought to come home to eat, Johnny. It ain't good eatin' around like that all the time. Besides, it costs a lot of money."

"It saves a lot of time, Ma. I got a lot of things to take care of." He looked over to the bedroom door then. "What's Stella doin', sleepin'?" He went over and looked in the door. "What's the matter, Stell? Ain't you glad to see me?"

"Come in here, Johnny. And close the door," I heard her say real low. Johnny shrugged and winked at me and went in. I tried to wink back, but I don't think it came off. I just sat there, watching Ma as she started to iron again. I hoped I wouldn't get dragged into it, but I figured I would

I could hear their voices in the bedroom, but they weren't very loud. I couldn't understand what they said, but I hoped she wasn't saying anything about the letter to Johnny. Ma didn't seem to pay any attention, though, so I picked up the magazine. I turned the pages, looking at the ads, but I hardly saw what they were about. I was too nervous, just sitting there. .pa

I wished I could hear them, and at the same time I was sure glad I couldn't. All of a sudden, then, I heard Stella cry out, almost like a scream. I jumped up but

Ma kept on ironing. She looked at me, but didn't say anything. I felt like a fool and sat down.

The door opened then, and Johnny came back in the kitchen. He walked over to me, looking pretty mad.

"Look, kid, I told you before an' I'll tell you again. What goes on between me and Stella is my business, not even hers. You keep your nose out, do you hear?"

"She asked me an' I told her, that's all. I thought you was goin' to tell her you tore up her letter." I said that loud so Ma would know what was going on. "It was her letter, so I told her, that's all."

"I was goin' to tell her when I got good an' ready. It's nobody's business but mine. All you got to think about's gettin' that barn fixed up. Don't think about anythin' else, you hear?" He wasn't yelling, but he sure was pretty mad. I didn't know what to say, so I just sat there. And Ma kept on ironing.

Stella came into the kitchen then, but Johnny didn't even look at her. "Get back in the bedroom," he said.

She just stood there. "I tried to be quiet about this and explain to you how I felt. But you don't understand anything like that, do you?" She rubbed her face then, and I saw her cheek was all red. I figured then I knew why she cried out like she did.

"Stella, I'm takin' care of this. I know what's best."

"My friends aren't good enough for me, is that the reason?" She faced right up to him. "You're going to find me some better ones, perhaps? Are you? Or is it that you can't stand me having anything to do with any-one but you? Is that the reason? Are you scared, Johnny, so scared deep down inside so that you've got to be tough, got to make people afraid of you, hate you, even?"

"Shut up," Johnny said and raised his hand like he was going to hit her. "An' get in there where you belong."

"I've said all I've got to say anyway." She turned away. "You win. I'll shut up. And I won't write any more letters." She went into the bedroom and closed the door.

Ma came over then and stood looking at Johnny. he sort of flushed and turned away, but Ma put her hand on his arm. "Johnny, I ain't goin' to interfere or tell you what you should do."

"All right, then, Ma, don't." He jerked his arm away. "You ain't got no right to butt in, either. This is between me and Stella. And Bobby, 'cause he butted in." He turned again to me. "All I want out of you is some results in that barn, do you hear? And get the old man out there with you. We ain't got forever. I'll tell him myself, if you ain't got the guts."

"Johnny," Ma said.

"I know what I'm doin'."

"Johnny, you got to take care..."

"Leave me alone, Ma. Just leave me alone." Johnny went into the bedroom and closed the door. Ma looked after him a minute and then went back to her ironing. I just sat there. I didn't know what else to do. For a second I thought I heard Stella crying, but I couldn't be sure. That night, though, I dreamed that she did until I got her to stop.

Chapter 8

I never liked to work with Pa much because it was
harder to keep even with him than it was to do things
yourself, but because Johnny said I had to, I did. Inside
of two weeks, though, we had the barn pretty well in
shape for a stock room, as we began to call it. We
burned more old stuff than even Pa knew we had, and
piled more--stuff we could sell like scrap metal--out behind the barn. We used what lumber we had and built
shelves along the back wall. When Johnny came in to
look one day, he said they would do for small parts.
Most of the time, though, he was off somewhere in my
truck, looking for junk cars, he said. George Hite was
always with him. Once in a while they'd tow an old
wreck home, using the truck.

They had four old cars lined up in the pasture, a
model A Ford, two old Chevies, and a thirty-nine Plymouth. With those, and a big bonfire going most of the
time, and a pile of scrap iron behind the barn, the
place was beginning to look like a junkyard. Pa was
kind of proud of it, I guess, especially of the big sign
that Johnny and George Hite put up. Lust and Hite
Auto Wrecking, the big letters said, and then underneath, Used Parts. It was a nice sign. They had it
painted special.

"Just goes to show, a man can do damn near anything he's got a mind to in this country," Pa said one
morning when he came into the barn. It was after nine,
and I'd been working for over an hour, but he'd been
off somewhere since right after breakfast. Johnny'd

given him some money the day before, and as I walked over to him, I could smell the cheap whiskey he must of bought with it.

"Where's the booze, Pa?" I asked him, wondering where he'd got it. He couldn't of been into town.

"That Hite boy is sure a fine feller. People certainly have that boy wrong." He sat down on a bench we'd made. "Yes sir, when two fine boys get together, there ain't much they can't do."

"Pa, you know you ain't supposed to drink. That's why you got bad kidneys." I sat down beside him, feeling kind of foolish. It was the only pleasure the old man had, and it hadn't kiled him yet.

"Yes sir, it makes a man feel good in his old age," he said, taking a pint bottle out of his pocket. It was half-empty.

"What, Pa, the booze?" I was trying to be funny.

"You just never mind." He sounded a little mad. "If you had half the get-up your brother's got, you wouldn't be plaguin' your old father. You'd be out doin' things.

"I didn't mean anything, Pa. You got a right to drink.

"You're God damn right I got a right to drink." he shook the bottle at me, slopping a little whiskey out.

I got up off the bench and went over to where I'd been sawing a board. He followed me over. I picked up the saw again. I figured he'd wander off somewheres.

"You always been a sullen one, too good for your old man. But now things is goin' to be different."

I didn't pay any attention, but he was making me a little sore. I started to saw where I'd marked. It was a hard board, and I ignored Pa. It made him madder. He kind of grabbed at the saw.

"You put down that saw. I'm layin' down the law."

I went on sawing. he took a swing at me that missed a mile, and he almost fell. I quit sawing and turned around. He straightened up and was breathing pretty hard.

"Pa, cut it out. Why don't you go over and sit down? I got a lot of work to do."

"You shut up." He pushed at me and I stepped back.

"Cut it out, Pa. I'm tellin' you."

"You ain't tellin' nobody nothin'." There was spit running down the corner of his mouth. Suddenly I got mad, more at that than anything else, I guess.

"Pa, shut up." I stepped up to him. "I'm getting sick of it. I ain't never raised my hand to you yet, but by God, if you don't, I'm goin' to, right now." He looked at me a minute and then looked away. There were big tears in his eyes. I turned away and picked up the saw again. I wasn't mad anymore and I felt pretty lousy. After a minute or two he went outside, and I went on sawing. I worked alone after that. Pa didn't come into the barn anymore, and he didn't have much to say to me up at the house. If he ever told Johnny about it, Johnny never let on.

Chapter 9

At first I figured Pa was just as glad that I'd got mad at him, because then he'd have a good excuse for not working in the barn. Not that Pa needed any excuse for anything anymore, except maybe to himself. Anyway, I didn't miss him much because we didn't do any talking or kidding around like fellows do when they're working, and he always made me feel kind of uncomfortable, like he thought I wasn't much good at working or at figuring things out.

One afternoon a couple of days later, as I was carrying some trash out to the fire, I noticed Pa standing off a little ways, looking around, first at the cars and then at the barn and the big sign. It seemed like he was reading the sign over to himself a couple of times. He made like he didn't see me, but how could he help it? After a minute or so, he went around the corner of the barn, walking slow and looking down at the ground like he might of lost something.

While I was standing there watching the fire so's none of the stuff would blow around and maybe start the barn on fire, I wondered what the hell Pa was hanging around for. I thought it real tough, too, because I knew he wasn't going to bother me anymore like he used to. I figured I let him know I was a man now even if he wasn't anymore. As I went back to the barn, though, I wasn't so sure, and I didn't feel so tough as I thought about it. Pa was an old man, and he wasn't much good to anybody, not even himself, but still he was Pa. And I knew I was grown up even if Pa didn't. I had no right spoiling what little Pa had to make himself feel as though he was something.

That was the trouble with all of us, I figured, or at least all of us except Ma. We was all trying to be something, at least to ourselves. We couldn't stand it if we had to admit we was nothing and couldn't be anything but nothing no matter how we tried. Either we didn't have it in us to be something or else we didn't get a break or else it was both. Maybe for me and Pa it was both. For Johnny and Stella, I wasn't so sure. They were both pretty smart. Maybe Johnny was right, saying you had to make your own breaks. And you had to admit, this time he was really trying, starting a junk yard while cars and parts were so hard to get. I sure hoped right then it would work out. Maybe it would turn out to be the break we all needed. Maybe if it did, things would start to be different.

Still, all the time I was working, I couldn't shake the idea of Pa going around the barn like he had something to do. Pa always used to have something to do and had plenty of plans, way back when I was a kid. I couldn't help wondering what he saw when he looked up at the sign. I got to wishing for a minute that I hadn't come out of the barn and made him go off the way he did. I could remember a long time ago when Pa wouldn't of had to go off like that. He would of stood there and said what he thought.

Every so often when I was pretty young, Pa used to like to go off in the woods. He had a dog and a gun, and sometimes he'd bring home a rabbit or woodchuck or even a pheasant. In the winter sometimes he'd set out some traps, and once in a while, he'd take me along. Pa liked to talk in those days, and he taught me a lot about the woods and how the wild things got along, shifting for food and keeping alive.

One time in the middle of winter I remember Pa taking me along when he went out to look after his traps. It was early in the morning, and it was really cold. There was a light, powdery snow on the ground that crunched when you walked. Pa made us walk slow so we wouldn't get up a sweat. He said that was how you caught cold if you didn't watch yourself.

We walked along the creek bank through the pasture and back toward the woods. Pa walked on the high ground, like an Indian, he said, and he made me do the same. Just before we got to the woods, we saw a line of tracks in the snow. I figured they were made by a dog, but Pa got all excited.

"Look, Bobby, look. By jingoes, we got a fox around here."

I looked, but I couldn't see any difference. Besides, my feet were getting cold. "Looks like old Spot to me, Pa."

"Those tracks was made by a fox." Pa grinned like an owl.

"How can you tell, Pa? I can't see any difference."

"When you been around as much as I have, you just know. You got to watch an' study things out." He bent over to look at them close. "It ain't hard, once you get the feel."

"What's foxes good for, Pa?" I started to jump up and down.

"Now stop that, Bobby. You know better than to scare the critters like that. An' I don't want to scare that fox till I get me a stronger trap than I got."

I stopped jumping. "What they good for, Pa?"

"Why this old fox is worth five dollars if I catch him. Besides, they sure raise hell with the chickens."

"Think he's been gettin' any of ours, Pa?"

"Nope, none of ours yet. I watch 'em pretty close." Pa stood up then. "No tellin' when he's goin' to try, though. But now we know about him, he ain't goin' to get a chance." He looked around for a minute where the tracks cut out toward the woods. "No sense followin' him today. But we'll get that bugger, now we know he's around."

"We sure will, Pa. We'll get him, all right." I felt some of Pa's excitement, I guess, because I didn't feel cold anymore. Besides, I'd never saw a fox except in pictures, and I knew they were pretty fierce. But Pa would fix him, I figured. I guess Pa thought so, too, because when we started off again, he was whistling low through his teeth.

We crossed the fence into the woods, and Pa started climbing down the creek bank to look at his traps. A couple of them were sprung and the bait was gone, and all of them were empty. he didn't say much to me, but he blamed it all on the fox. I didn't see any tracks around any of them but Pa said the fox took the bait before the snow fell. As we left the creek to swing around to a pond where Pa had his last trap, he really swore at the fox. He'd been figuring on getting at least a couple of muskrat pelts he could sell for fifty cents a piece.

We cut through an open place in the woods where there was a lot of rabbit tracks in the snow. We kicked up a couple out of the brush where they were sitting, and I threw snowballs at them as they ran for more cover. They sure looked funny jumping through the snow, and even Pa laughed. He seemed to of forgot about the fox.

"Sure wish we'd brought my gun along, on' old Spot. I should of thought they'd be out this mornin' lookin' for grub."

"Sure wish you had, too, Pa. i could shoot 'em myself."

"You're pretty young to use my shotgun. I'll be gettin' you one of your own one of these days." Pa spit on the snow.

"Will you, Pa? When, do you think?" I watched the brown spot spread where Pa spit. I was all excited.

"You got a lot of things to learn first. Like skinnin' an' cleanin' your game, an' preservin' the pelts. Besides, I'll have to get a little money, first. I'll get us that fox."

"I'll learn it all, Pa. You just watch. I'll help you skin that old fox." I was still all excited, but I wasn't so sure as I was anymore. I'd never shot anything, but once I killed a bird with a stone. I felt pretty bad, and I tried to patch it up, but it was dead. I buried it under the pear tree, and I never told anyone. And now if Pa got me a gun, I'd have to kill rabbits and things. Besides, I hated to watch Pa skin and clean things, and I always wanted to vomit when I saw the insides laying there on a paper before Pa give them to the dogs. I didn't think

I could get over that. Still, it'd be nice to have a gun of my own, and I'd probably get used to the rest of it.

We came to the pond then, and there were fox tracks all over in the snow. Pa got pretty mad again, and started to swear at the fox. I got pretty excited, and Pa did, too, when we heard something bark, sharper than a dog.

"Pa, what's that? Is that the fox, Pa?" I started to jump again.

"Take it easy, boy," he kind of yelled at me. "That's the fox, all right, an' it sounds like he's in trouble. I'm goin' around an' look at our trap." He started to run around the pond, and I took off after him. Pa stopped then.

"You wait here. I'll yell if it's okay for you to come closer an' look."

"Okay, Pa," I said, but I came on anyway, slower than before.

In a minute, I heard Pa yell again. He was down in the gulley where he always set his trap. The fox barked again, like he was mad more than he was hurt, and Pa yelled, "Quick, Bobby, get me a club or somethin'." He sure was excited.

I looked around quick, but I couldn't see anything, so I ran up to the gulley. There was a skinny red fox with his front foot caught in the trap, and Pa was standing a few feet away, trying to kick at him. But everytime Pa got close the fox would snap at him, and Pa'd have to get back. When Pa heard me, he looked up and almost lost his balance, the gulley was so narrow and steep. Then he swore again.

"I couldn't find anythin', Pa," I yelled, excited at seeing the fox. I never saw one up close before.

"Goddamnit, find an old piece of lumber or somethin'. This trap ain't goin' to hold out much longer. It's too light."

I looked around again, but I couldn't see anything except a big round stone half-covered with snow. I could hardly lift it, but I got it over to the edge of the gulley. When I looked down, Pa was still trying to kick the fox, and the fox was pulling on the chain that held the trap, trying to get loose. If I wouldn't of been so excited, I would of felt sorry for him, but all I could think of was getting him like Pa said.

"Here, Pa," I yelled. "Here's a big rock. Maybe you can get him with this." Just then I dropped the rock, and it rolled down the side of the gulley, almost hitting Pa. Pa fell down and the rock bounced off something and up in the air. I thought it was going to hit the fox, and I held my breath. But it hit the stake that the trap was chained to, and the stake snapped like a gun. Pa jumped up and yelled and tried to kick the fox again, but the fox started to run up the side of the gulley, dragging the trap, stumbling when the chain or the trap caught in some brush. Then he'd pull it free and run till it caught again, but he got to the top of the gulley. Pa climbed up after him as fast as he could, but by the time Pa got up there, the fox was running across the field toward the woods, limping and dragging the chain behind him. Pa ran after him a little ways, and then turned around and came back up to me. I was still pretty excited, and I was kind of glad that the fox got away. I watched till he got into the woods, and Pa just stood there, not saying anything. Then I remembered how bad Pa wanted to catch the fox.

"Geez, Pa, I didn't mean to let him get away."

"I know you didn't, Bobby. It was just the breaks is all. But a fox. A five-dollar hide. An' he got away." Then he grinned for a minute. "There's a chance he might get hung up somewheres on some brush. Think I'll track him awhile. Like to get the trap back, anyway." He started off across the field, and then turned to me. "You better stay here, Bobby. I won't be gone any longer'n I can help."

"Okay, Pa. I won't go away." This time I meant it, and I hoped for Pa's sake that he'd catch that old fox.

I got pretty cold, just standing there waiting, but I figured it was no more than I deserved. I just stared down in the gulley, where the snow was all beat down and there were spots of blood all over from the fox, and the big rock laying there where it broke off the stake. I felt pretty bad, but I didn't know who ought to win, Pa or the fox.

It was about an hour, I guess, before Pa came back out of the woods, swinging his trap. For a minute I figured he'd caught up with the fox. Then when I could see his face I knew that he didn't.

"Damn old fox slipped the trap like I figured he would."

"Did you catch up to him, Pa?"

"Nope. No tellin' where he is now, in the next county, I guess. But I'm goin' to get me a big trap, an' I'll get him yet."

We headed for home then, after Pa re-set the trap. We didn't talk much, and I felt sorry for Pa. He did get a bigger trap, and he set it, but we never saw sign of the fox. All Pa would bring home was once in a while a muskrat or coon. I felt pretty bad whenever I thought about it because it was my fault Pa didn't get the fox. Still, he always figured he would, and he never said anything to me about being mad.

I sure wished Pa hadn't changed, that he'd got the fox and a break with his farming and his jobs and now with his back. or with his kids, too, I figured, especially me. Once right after I bought the truck, he asked me to use it and I said no. And now, after getting mad at him in the barn, he was going off pretending he was looking for something. I felt pretty lousy, but what could I do? Anyway, Pa never came in the barn again while I was working. Still, once in a while I'd see him out looking at the sign.

Chapter 10

Working in the barn all by myself kept me pretty busy, but it wasn't the kind of work that gave you much to think about. It wasn't like sitting at the stitching machine at the box factory, where you had to watch every minute to get the staples in right. i wished Johnny or even George Hite would stay around and help, mainly so's I'd have somebody to talk to, but when I asked Johnny once, he said they had too much to do. It made me kind of mad, even if he was boss, but there wasn't much I could do about it except work by myself. it wasn't much fun, except that nobody was around to tell me what do do. That helped quite a bit.

I kind of thought it would be nice if Stella came around once in a while, just to keep me company, but she never did. Once, though, when I looked out the door I saw her up by the house, laying in the sun with a bathing suit on. I watched her for quite a while, and I sure figured Johnny was lucky. He really got a break, even if he didn't act like he knew it sometimes. She really looked good, with her black hair down her back and a bathing suit on.

After a while, though, I saw Ma come out of the house and go over to where Stella was laying. Ma said something, I couldn't hear what, and then Stella got up. It looked like they were arguing or something, but after a minute, Stella picked up her blanket and went into the house.

I wished Ma didn't have to be like that, always making out like things were bad, even Stella laying in the sun. But then, maybe Ma was smarter than any of us knew. Maybe she figured I was watching from the barn, thinking the things I was thinking. But I couldn't see anything bad in it, even in thinking like I was. I remembered Pa saying a long time ago, a woman was made to be looked at. I didn't know what he meant till I met Stella.

I remembered when he said it, though, at supper one night. He was kidding Johnny about being big enough to go to the hootch show at the carnival that was playing in town. Johnny kind of stuttered and giggled, and Pa laughed at him and so did I. We were having a good time until Ma came over to the table. Everyone kind of shut up then except me. I guess I didn't know any better.

"You think the ladies in tights'd really like Johnny, Pa?" I said, still laughing at the idea.

Ma put a dish down on the table. "Joe Lust, what're you tellin' these boys?" She sounded kind of mad.

"We was just havin' a little fun with Johnny, Ma," Pa said.

"He was tellin' us about the ladies in the carnival and how they'd really go for Johnny with his slicked-back hair," I piped up, kind of giggling. Pa gave me a look and I shut up.

Ma just stood there looking at Pa for a minute. Johnny and I started to eat real fast. We were having noodle soup.

"Ma, you know how boys go on about such things," Pa said like it was nothing. He started to eat, too.

"Joe Lust, you've said an' done a lot of things, an' I never said nothin' about them. But I ain't goin' to let you fill these boys' minds with the filth that you like to drag home all the time. I ain't goin' to put up with it."

"Christ, Ma, we was just kiddin' around," Pa said with his mouth full. Ma really seemed to get mad then.

"You ain't goin' to ruin these boys. I'd sooner see 'em dead, or you, or me dead than to let you go on the way you have been ever since we been married. If you'd think about somethin' good, like goin' to church or even prayin' once in a while, maybe things'd be different."

Pa said something else then, but I didn't hear it. All I could think of was what she said about seeing us dead. Johnny didn't seem to mind, and he even winked at me, but I was sure scared. Ma sounded like she meant it, even if I couldn't see anything wrong.

Johnny piped up then. He kind of grinned as he looked up at Ma. "What's so bad about lookin' at ladies, Ma? They sure act like they like men to look at 'em."

"You shut up! Never talk like that again. You're callin' down the judgement of the Lord on all of us."

"I don't see why, Ma. He made us this way." Johnny sounded real innocent, but I could tell he was doing it to plague Ma. Pa gave Johnny a look, but Johnny didn't pay any attention. Then Pa reached over and slapped Johnny in the face, just about knocking Johnny off his chair. Johnny yelled, but he didn't really sound hurt, and Ma grabbed Pa's arm. She held onto Pa while he tried to shake her off. In a minute, though, he just sat there, his face all red. Johnny was crying, holding his hand to his face where Pa hit him. I just sat there, breathing hard, looking down at his plate.

"You fool," Ma said, "you poor old fool. To think you can put your own sins off on a boy. You fill 'em full of your foolishness, what can you expect but to get it right back?" She turned to Johnny then and put her hand on his head. "It's all right, son. You got to consider the source."

"I didn't do anything, Ma. All I said was what Pa said." Johnny kept on crying, although it sounded kind of put on to me.

"I know, son," Ma said. She went away from the table then.

After a minute Pa pushed his chair away from the table and without saying anything, he got up and went outside. I didn't feel like eating any more soup, and I felt kind of sick to my stomach, but Johnny made some sort of crack and then started to eat again. I wouldn't even look at him, but just sat there for a while. Then I got up and started to go outside. Ma must of seen me then.

"Sit down and finish your soup, Bobby." She sounded tired.

"I ain't hungry, Ma." I kept on going, and she didn't say any more.

Pa was outside, sitting on the wellstone, just looking off across the fields. I wanted to go over and sit down next to him, but I didn't. I just stood there, trying to figure out why Pa was so wrong and Ma was so right. It seemed like everything that was funny or that gave you a jumpy feeling inside was no good. I couldn't figure it out.

Pa looked up at me and then looked away again. "Go back in the house," he said. "You ain't got no business out here."

I just stood there, and Pa looked at me again. "You hear what I say? Go on now, git out of here. Your Ma won't like it if you hang around me. Go on back into the house."

I wanted to say something, but I didn't know what. And I didn't want to stay if Pa didn't want me, and I didn't want to go back in the kitchen and watch Johnny eating his soup. Pa got up then and started to walk down the lane. He didn't look back.

Ma stuck her head out the door then. "Bobby, you get back in here and finish your supper. Never mind your Pa."

I looked after Pa. He didn't look back. "Okay, Ma," I said after a minute and went back in. I couldn't eat any more soup, though, and I never liked it since. Johnny finished mine that night.

Ma made us go to bed not long after supper, like she did once in a while when she wanted us out of the way. Johnny didn't seem to care, but I didn't want to go 'cause I wanted to see Pa. But he didn't come in, so I laid on the bed and tried to go to sleep even if Johnny did keep the light on. After a while, we heard Pa come in. Johnny got up and went over by the door to listen. He was grinning like it was funny, and he motioned to me to come over. I wouldn't go right then, but after a minute I did. I knew that kind of thing was wrong, but right then I didn't care. I was thinking about Pa.

I couldn't hear anything at first and then after a while, Pa said, "Okay. You win. I'll leave you alone if that's what you want. But you didn't have to do what you did in front of the boys."

"'Bout time they saw how nasty you are." I could almost picture Ma as she said it, standing with her hands on her hips, seeming bigger than Pa.

"Good God, I'm a man, ain't I?" Pa sounded tired.

"If you was a man, you'd act like one. Do the things a man's supposed to do, like workin' an' providin' and leavin' off the swearing. An' makin' like you're somethin' more than a bull in a pasture full of cows." I could still picture Ma. I wasn't sure what she meant, but I felt sorry for Pa, mostly because he didn't say much, like he knew he was wrong. I wanted to go to bed, but at the same time I wanted to listen. Once in a while Johnny'd look at me and grin, like he was enjoying it. But I just felt kind of dirty.

We could hear them moving around and pretty soon the door to the front room opened and we didn't hear anything for a long time. I was just going back to bed when I heard Ma say "Leave me alone", real sharp. Pa said something that sounded like "All right", and that was all.

When we got back in bed, Johnny started making fun, especially of Pa, by grabbing at me and then saying, "Cut it out." I didn't like it, and I got pretty mad, but I pretended I thought it was funny, so he quit. If I'd let him know I was mad, he wouldn't of let up.

It was about that time that Pa quit talking much about things, not even to me or to Johnny, and he didn't go out in the woods much anymore. He rented most of the farm to Bill Glen, and when I asked him once about trapping again, he said it was in the agreement the game belonged to Bill Glen. He just sat around, or would go off into town, or would get a job for a while. But he never talked much to Ma, and she didn't say much to him.

After a while, I got to looking at Pa just as Pa, hanging around, and never thought much about him at all till I saw him going around the side of the barn like he had something to do.

Like I said, working around an old barn gives you plenty of time to think, especially when you get all sweated up and have to stop and rest. It's not too good, either, because when you think too much you get to figuring what's the use because you can't make things come out right anyway. Or you can't change things that are over and done with.

Every once in a while that whole afternoon, whenever I'd remember Stella out in her bathing suit, I'd go over and look, but she didn't come out anymore. I figured Ma told her it was wrong, and so she wouldn't do it any more, but I couldn't help wondering. The sun was supposed to be good, but if you went out to lay in it, you were doing wrong. I couldn't see how Ma could tell I was watching, anyway. And I didn't mean any harm, even by thinking what I was. Stella was just something to look at was all.

After a while I got tired and went in the house. Ma was getting supper fixed. I sat down on the couch and after a while, I asked, kind of casual, "Where's Stella, Ma?" In takin' a nap?" Ma shook her head. "I don't know, Bobby, I don't know."

"Ain't she home, Ma?" I said, kind of loud.

"Yeah, she's home," Ma said. "She must be takin' a nap."

I didn't say any more then, but I went outside where it was cool. I figured it would be nice if Stella'd come out so we could talk. But she didn't, and pretty soon Ma called me for supper. Stella ate, but she didn't talk much at all, and didn't even bow her head when Ma said the prayer. I figured I had a pretty good idea of what Ma said to her, but I still didn't let on. I figured if I got a chance, I'd tell her Ma didn't mean anything. But after supper she went in the bedroom and closed the door. I sat around hoping she'd come out till I got sleepy and went to bed. I was so tired I never even heard Johnny come in.

Chapter II

At breakfast the next day, Johnny was in a pretty good mood, talking about a junkyard him and George Hite went to see in Toledo. It was the kind of operation he said he wanted to run, with plenty of stock and a regular store room to sell parts, and what he said he liked best of all, a car-rebuilding department, where they'd take wrecked cars and fix them up and paint them like new. That was where the money was, Johnny said, because guys coming home from the army had plenty of money saved up, and they all wanted to buy cars. They didn't much care how much they had to pay for them either, he said.

It sounded pretty good to me because the way Johnny told it, I could almost see how we could have it if things worked out all right. Even Pa sat there grinning, kind of nodding his head once in a while. Ma just sat there, though, looking as if she really wasn't listening. But as I listened to him, I knew why Stella really married Johnny. He really could talk when he wanted to.

Johnny started to eat his pancakes real fast then, before they got cold, and I sat there thinking how smart he was to figure it all out and make it sound so easy.

"You think we can do all that, Johnny, get into the car rebuilding business, too? It's goin' to take a lot of money."

"We ain't got the money, kid, but we got a place, and for a lot of it we can use hard work instead. As soon as we get going, we'll be on our way."

"But how we going to fix up wrecked cars? We ain't got the stuff, an' we sure don't know enough about it."

"George Hite knows cars, I tell you. An' he can teach us. Hell, this car business is goin' to be the part that really pays off, once we get started. As long as the shortage holds out, anyway, an' even after, pro'bly." He was chewing pancakes while he talked, and it didn't sound so easy or so good this time. I still kind of wondered.

Johnny pushed his chair away from the table then and got up. He stood there picking his teeth with a match for a minute. "Well, I got to get goin'. We're goin' to look for a chain fall to lift heavy parts today. I got a lead on one, I think." He looked down at me then. "Once we get goin' good, I'll have George overhaul your old truck. We'll fix it up like new for you."

If it's still got enough pieces left by then, I thought, but I didn't say anything, just nodded my head and kept on eating.

Ma looked up at Johnny then. "Where you off to today, son?"

"I told you, Ma. I got to look for a chain fall."

"Does it always have to take all day an' half the night?"

"Sure it does, Ma. Sometimes it takes more than that."

"Some of the ladies from church said you was in a beer joint the other day. That ain't the way to do things."

Johnny grinned. "How'd they know unless they was themselves?"

Ma made like she didn't hear that. "It ain't right to go off like that, leavin' Stella by herself. You ought to be stayin' with her more. After all, she's your wife."

"She's in good hands, Ma. You'll keep her on the straight and narrow."

"I didn't mean that. That doesn't keep you out of beer joints."

"Hell, that's the way business is run these days, Ma. You make a deal, you got to have a drink after. That's all."

Pa spoke up then. "You just leave the boy alone, Ma. He knows what he's doin'. You got to get along an' do like other people if you want to get any place."

"Like you been doin' all these years? You never mind. I know what's right an' what ain't. Johnny better listen to me."

The way it sounded, Ma let on like Johnny was a little kid. I hoped he'd go on out before he got mad. But he didn't seem to get mad, just stood there chewing the toothpick.

"Pa's right, Ma. I know what I'm doin'. I ain't goin' to get in any trouble. I know better'n that. I'm no kid anymore."

"It ain't enough just to keep out of trouble. You got to live right, too."

"What do you call livin' right, Ma?" Johnny gave one of his mean laughs. "Like this, all my life? Don't make me laugh."

I started to get up 'cause I didn't want to hear any more. Whenever Johnny got like that, I started to get scared. But Ma gave me a look like she wanted me to stay, so I sat down again.

"Now listen to me, Johnny. I ain't never scolded you much. I guess I should of, but I didn't. As long as you're under this roof, I ain't goin' to let you go on like this."

"I got to go, Ma. You can tell me some other time." He started to go around the table, but Ma grabbed his arm.

"Now you listen to me." She sounded pretty sharp, like I hadn't heard her in a long time. I wished I'd of gone out.

"I told you, Ma. I ain't got the time." Johnny tried to pull his arm loose, but she held on. "Look, Ma," he said. "You better let go before I get sore. You can tell me tonight."

He started to go toward the door again, pulling Ma along. I knew it wasn't right, but I didn't know what to say. I didn't blame Johnny, and I didn't blame Ma, either. It was one of those things. So what could I do?

Ma kind of let her hands drop then, and Johnny stopped for a minute. He turned to Ma then and said, kind of soft, "It's okay, Ma. Just don't fret. You got your ways an' I got mine. That's all. I know you mean right, but I got to do things my way, is all."

"Your way!" Ma really spit it out at him. "You ain't goy any way. Gone all the time an' comin'in all hours, smellin' of beer, an' then goin' ion the room to her and carryin' on all night like a couple of dogs. I know what's goin' on. You ain't foolin' me none."

"You leave Stella out of this, I'm tellin' you." Johnny got mad.

"Better if you'd of left her out of it. I tried to teach you to do right. I guess maybe I didn't try hard enough."

"You leave Stella out of it. You ain't got nothin' to say about it, anyway. It's nobody's business but mine." He sounded like he was cooling off again. Johnny never stayed mad very long. "Just don't let it bother you, Ma. It doesn't make any difference what we do in the long run, anyway. Nothin' really matters." Before Ma could say anything else, he went out the door without even looking at her. Ma just stood there a minute, looking after him, and then she turned to Pa.

"How can you set there and let him go off like that? But you never cared anyway, about anything 'cept yourself." She turned away without giving Pa a chance to answer and went over to the sink. Pa just sat there, acting like he didn't know what was going on.

I finished my pancakes even though they were cold and sat there drinking my coffee. Times like that I sure wished Johnny'd stayed in the army or something. It wasn't so bad around before he came home. At least nobody bothered anybody else, and we got along.

Just as I finished my coffee, Stella came into the room. She was tying her robe around her. It was made out of some shiny black stuff that just matched her hair. If things hadn't been such a mess I sure would of been glad to see her. She sat down at the table and smiled at Pa and me and said, "Good morning." We both said it back, and then Ma brought some more pancakes over from the stove and put them on the platter. Stella said, "Good morning, Ma," but Ma didn't even look at her, just went back to the stove.

Stella gave me a wink then. I figured she was making fun of Ma so I looked away, but then she said, "What was all the arguing about this morning? It's hard for a girl to sleep." I looked back at her and she was smiling, but her eyes looked kind of hard. I glanced at Ma. She was still over by the stove.

"Wasn't really anythin', Stella," I said. "We was just having a little discussion."

"You certainly believe in forceful discussions. I thought Johnny was going to tear the door off when he left."

"Johnny's just full of fun, Stella. You know how he is."

"He certainly is. Like all the rest of you, so full of fun he keeps it all to himself, afraid someone is going to snatch it away from him or tell him it'll make him sick." All of a sudden she quit smiling, and her voice dropped, just as Pa started to laugh. She kind of blushed and then she said, "I didn't mean it, Bobby. I guess I'm not very funny in the morning."

"It's okay," I told her. "I guess nobody is."

"It's just that..." She jumped up from her chair. "I guess I'm not very hungry this morning." She ran in the bedroom and closed the door.

Pa looked at me then. "What in the hell is the matter with her?" He picked up his cup and poured the coffee down his throat like he does.

"I don't know, Pa," I said, getting up. I kind of thought maybe working alone wasn't so bad after all. At least you knew where you stood with nobody else around. You knew what was coming off. I picked up a cold pancake to eat on my way down to the barn.

"Ma, I got to get goin' down to the barn," I said, just to have something to say to her.

She came over to the table then. "Their carryin' on half the night is goin' to bear fruit." She kind of smiled to herself.

"It ain't that, Ma," I said, taking a bite of pancake so"s I wouldn't have to say anything else right then. But Ma looked at me kind of funny.

"Ain't it?" she said like she knew better. "Serves her right, too." I went on out. I wondered how Ma could think it was that simple.

For a change it was good to get back to the barn. I had some cupboards to build for tools and parts, and I figured it would keep me busy enough because it had to be done just right. I always liked to measure and fit things together anyway.

By noontime I had the cupboards pretty well up except the doors, bnd I had to wait till Johnny brought home some hinges before I could fix them, so I went up to the house. I didn't feel much like going in, but I did, and Stella was in the kitchen, setting the table. She was all fixed up in a dress and looked pretty good.

"You're a little early, Bobby. Lunch isn't ready yet."

"It's okay. I guess I'll get a little air first then. It's pretty stuffy in that old barn." I looked around the kitchen, wondering where Ma and Pa were, but I didn't see them. Then I heard Ma say something in the other room. I started to go out.

.pa

"Sit down, Bobby. It won't be long."

"I been cooped up all morning. I'll sit down outside."

"Wait a minute, Bobby. I want to apologize for being such a fool this morning. I don't know what made me talk that way."

"You didn't say anythin'", I told her, feeling kind of funny about it.

"You knew what I meant. And I'm sorry."

"Don't worry about it." I grinned then. "Ma thought you were pregnant."

Stella giggled then. "She didn't! Whatever made her think that?"

"You runnin' off the way you did, I guess." The way Stella was laughing at it, I felt a lot better.

"Doesn't she think I know any better," she said, still kind of giggling. Then she got serious all of a sudden. "Maybe I should. You're supposed to when you get married, and maybe I'd like to. If only you could be sure."

"You can't be sure of anythin'. People ain't made that way."

"I know. I guess that's the trouble. I thought I was sure when we first got married, but I'm not anymore."

"It's this place, ain't it, Stella? I kind of thought it wouldn't work out when Johnny wrote he was bringin' you home."

"It's not that, Bobby. The farm isn't what I expected, that, I'll admit. But it goes a lot beyond that. It's us, Johnny and me." She looked away and then back at me. "If only I could get close to him, talk to him, but he's built up such a shell. I wish I knew why." She looked at me a minute. "But he's not the only one. All of you have, Bobby, even you. I thought nothing would ever bother me as long as I didn't let it, but God, now I don't know."

She smiled at me then. "I guess I ought to keep my big mouth shut more often," she said.

"It's all right," I said, feeling like a fool. She kind of pointed out what was wrong with us, but I couldn't tell what it was that made us that way, or why. We just couldn't talk about anything real. Maybe it was a shell, like Stella said. Whatever it was, there was nothing you could do.

Ma came in the kitchen then and kind of looked at us standing so close together. I said something about forgetting to wash, and I went outside to the pump. I took my time washing, and when I came back in, they were all sitting at the table, It hit me all of a sudden I knew Stella better than I knew Pa or Ma. It kind of scared me for a minute, and then I looked at Pa.

"We're really gettin' the barn in shape, Pa. You ought to come down an' take a look. It don't look like the same old place." I grinned at him friendly like, hoping he'd see what I meant.

"I don't care. I got more important things to do," Pa said, picking up his fork. He looked down at his plate.

"It's real nice, Pa," I said right off, without thinking. "But it's kind of hard gettin' cupboards straight. Maybe you could come down an' help me line 'em up straight."

Pa didn't look up. He mumbled something like "Leave me alone," and started to eat. Something kind of grabbed me inside, and I turned quick to Ma, still grinning like a fool. I felt like I was naked.

"Ma, you ought to come down, too. You could give us some ideas-- about painting or somethin'."

"Eat your dinner, son. I got to get the dishes done."

I wanted to yell or laugh or cry or something, but I couldn't even move. Stella looked at me funny, and I rubbed my eye so she couldn't see how I felt. Then I started to eat as fast as I could. I wanted to get back to the barn.

Chapter 12

All during supper that night, Stella'd been talking about a movie she wanted to see that was playing in town. She sounded full of fun, like she wanted to show Ma she wasn't pregnant, but Johnny didn't take the hint. Most of the time he'd catch on to whatever she wanted, but tonight he didn't pay any attention. He didn't have too much to say and acted like he had something on his mind. I figured I knew what it was. There were eleven old cars in the pasture that him and George Hite must of paid ten or twenty dollars apiece for, and we hadn't sold any parts to amount to anything.

Still, Stella didn't seem to notice that Johnny was worried. After Pa went in the other room and Ma started to clean up the table, Stella went around and sat on his lap. She ran her fingers through his hair.

"Johnny, we haven't been to a movie or anyplace since we got here. And I really want to see this one," she whispered out loud.

He grinned, and his face kind of softened as he pulled her close. I got up and went over to my couch and picked up a catalog. I felt a little foolish. As I sat down, I glanced at them. Johnny was frowning again. I began thumbing through the catalog, but I couldn't help hearing. They acted like Ma or me wasn't around.

"Damnit, Stella, I've got too much to do. Tonight George and me got to see a man."

"You and that old junkyard. You could've stayed in Boston and got a job, but you had to come home and show 'em. Well, you haven't shown me yet, except that you can chase around after old cars."

"It takes a lot of work and contacts to start a business. Pretty soon things'll be different."

"Yeah. You'll have more old cars in the pasture, and I'll get more and more like..." She shut up suddenly as Ma began to rattle dishes in the dishpan, and then she went on. "Oh, Johnny, I didn't expect this. I don't know how much longer I can stand it."

"I told you it was pretty hardscrabble around here."

"Yes, but..." She got up off his lap. "It doesn't have to be unless you want it that way."

"I told you. Give me a year. That's all I ask."

"I don't want to wait a year. Not even a week. I want to start living again. I'm not used to this."

"I can't take you to the movies. Not tonight, if you ever want things to be different."

"That isn't the important thing."

"That's what you want, ain't it?"

"No...I don't know."

I heard her walk across the kitchen. When I looked up, she was over at the bench where Ma had her dishpan. She picked up a towel and didn't say any more but started to dry the dishes. I looked down at the catalog again. There was lots of fine huinting stuff in it, and I started to add up prices in my head, just to have something to do.

"Bobby?"

I looked up. "What, Johnny?"

"Want to do me a favor?"

"Sure."

"Got any money?"

I remembered the seventeen dollars. "No."

He grinned. "I haven't paid you back yet, have I?"

"No."

He took out his wallet, looked at it, and took out a bill. Then he walked over to me.

"How about takin' Stella to the movies tonight?" He held out the bill. It was a five and I wondered where he'd gotten it unless it was part of mine. But that must have been gone a long time ago.

"I don't know, Johnny. Ain't you goin' to use the truck?"

"No. George is gettin' a car. How about it?"

I didn't want to, but I didn't know what to say. Still, the movie was a good one, and if any of the guys I knew saw me with Stella, maybe they wouldn't look. And some of the girls. I took the bill. "Maybe she don't want to go with me."

"She will. Do her good." He laughed. "Only don't get any ideas," he said like it was funny.

"I won't, Johnny," I told him. The thought of sitting next to Stella all alone in the movie made me a little nervous, though. That was the part I didn't like. I remembered the time I sat beside a girl in the movie and then, after, I followed her until she ran up on a porch and into a house. I didn't mean anything, but a man came out and looked around, and I hid in the bushes. I just wanted to know her and talk to her, but I was afraid to do it again, and I didn't go to the movies much after that. It was too easy to think they were true.

Johnny went over to talk to Stella, and in a minute he came back. "She'll go, kid," he said.

"Okay, Johnny."

"You be careful."

"I'm a good driver."

He laughed, but it didn't sound as though he meant it. "That's not what I meant. Have a good time."

"Sure."

A car pulled up beside the house then and honked its horn. Johnny turned away and looked out the door.

"There's George. I got to go." He ran over and kissed Stella quick, and then went out.

As he got into the car, I looked out. I wondered whose car George Hite had, but I couldn't tell. I never saw that one before. After it turned around, I picked up the catalog again. It opened to the ladies' part, and I started to thumb toward the back, killing time till Stella was ready.

In a few minutes she came over, wiping her hands. "Want me to get all fixed up, Bobby? Real glamorous, so you'll be proud to take me?" She sounded happy, and I put the catalog down.

"If you want to," I said, thinking I would have to change, too, but hell. I liked overalls. They didn't bind a man so. Still, Stella was real pretty when she got dressed up in those sweaters she wore sometimes. Maybe we'd go in the drug store after. I didn't care if I spent the whole five dollars.

"Get all fixed up, Stella," I said. "I'll change, too."

"A real date," she said, laughing. "We'll really show 'em, won't we, Bobby?" She went into the bedroom and shut the door. "I won't be long," she called out as I started to unbutton my shirt.

Ma came over then and looked at me. "Son, I don't like it. No good'll come of it either."

"What, Ma?" I acted like it was nothing, and took my shirt off, so I could go outside and wash.

"You ought to know better than to go chasin' with a married woman."

"It ain't chasin', Ma. Just to a movie is all."

"That ain't the point. Her place is here, waitin' for Johnnty, even if he is out half the night. You want a woman to go with, you find your own. There's plenty of 'em around, God knows, an' most of 'em are no better than she is. But stay away from Johnny's."

"My God Ma, it was his idea." I went to the door. "Christ, it's only a movie. You'd think it was a . . ." I couldn't think of the word, so I went out and pumped some water in the pan. Ma kind of gave me the creeps sometimes. She could make breathing a sin if she didn't like the way you went at it. Still, I shouldn't of swore in front of her. Now she'd be up half the night praying for me, I thought. She wasn't in the kitchen when I went back in, so I put on my other clothes and picked up the catalog again. This time I looked at the ladies. I didn't even care if Ma saw me.

When Stella came out, I whistled like the fellows do, and she laughed and turned around so I could look at her.

"Well? Think you'll be proud of me?"

"Sure," I said as I got up. She was a good looking girl. Johnny could really pick them. I told her so, too, as we went out to the truck, and she laughed again like she like to hear it.

She didn't talk much on the way into town though, so I figured she was thinking of something else, and I didn't talk either. I was wishing Ma hadn't said what she did. She could make things that were nothing sound like they was bad. I let Stella off at the movie and then went to park. I wanted anybody standing around to see her wait and then go in with me, but nobody was there. It always works out like that for me. That's why the town kids laugh at me, I guess. Nothing works out.

The picture was in color, a musical one, with some funny parts and some sad ones, but everything, even the sad parts, was beautiful. I didn't look at Stella at all, and I kept telling myself it wasn't real. I was glad when it was over. Why do they have to do that to people when they know we have to go home when it's over?

When we got in the truck, Stella looked at me. "Did you like it?" she asked. "I really did." She sounded excited.

"Sure," I said, and started to drive off. I figured what was the sense in going to the drugstore, so I headed back toward the farm.

"Let's not go home yet, Bobby," she said after a while.

"Where else is there?" She didn't know about movies and I couldn't tell her. People have to find out themselves.

"Isn't there some place where there's music and people and . . ."

"There's a roadhouse up ahead, down the river road."

"Let's go there."

"Ma wouldn't like it."

"Oh, hang Ma! The way she looks at me sometimes, like I'm evil or something." She turned quick and looked at me. "I'm sorry, Bobby. I didn't mean it."

"It's all right," I told her.

"It's just that I want to live and I don't get a chance anymore." She didn't say any more, and turned to look out the window. I turned off on the river road and pulled in front of the roadhouse. There were a lot of cars parked around under the trees. I parked over on the side, away from the road.

It was a little place, in an old house set back from the road, and it was all outlined in red neon. A man named Red Beazly ran it. He came to town during the war, and there was talk of him being a shrewd operator, but I didn't pay much attention to it, 'cause whenever he saw me he always said "Hello" as nice as anyone. Still, I'd never been in there. It wasn't good, and besides, I was pretty young, and you had to be twenty-one. I remembered Stella was only eighteen, too. Maybe they wouldn't let us in, I thought as we went up to the door. I was a little scared.

You could hear noise and music, like there were a lot of people inside having a good time. Stella sort of hesitated and then went in. I followed right behind her. It was pretty dark inside, except for lights at one end, where the bar was, and a juke box, all lit up, over near the wall. We saw an empty table and sat down. I was warm, and I was glad I just wore a shirt instead of a

suit like some of the guys had on. A lot of people were
dancing.

Stella turned so she could watch the dancers, and
when the girl who waited on tables came, I ordered
beer for both of us. She brought two glasses and I paid,
and we sat there, sipping the beer once in a while, and
watching the people. It was too noisy for me, but Stella
liked it. Once, though, when a fellow asked her to
dance, she said no and he went off back to the bar.

I was just taking a drink of beer when a man came
along and stopped by the table. It was Mr. Beazly, and
he looked pretty serious. He was a goodlooking man,
not too old but not young either. He grinned like he
was trying to be friendly.

"Hi, Lust. Mind if I sit down?"

"No, sir," I said, and pushed the glass away.

"Pretty young to be drinking, aren't you?" He pulled
a chair up and sat down between us.

"We didn't mean anythin'. Just a glass of beer is all."

He laughed. "Hell, it's all right. Half the people in
here aren't twenty-one." He looked at Stella then.
"What's the matter with your girl? Can't she talk?"

"This is Stella, my brother's wife."

He looked at her again. "So you're Johnny's wife.
No wonder he's so anxious to get ahead, starting a business."

I wondered how he knew that, but I didn't ask. People always know everything around Titus anyway. he
moved his chair so he was facing Stella. I could only
see her arm, and it made me kind of mad. Johnny
would of hit him probably.

"Like to dance, Stella?" he asked her.

"No, thank you," she said right off, real polite, and took a sip of beer.

"I always like to get to know my guests."

"I imagine you do," she said, and he laughed.

"Well, if you change your mind, I like to dance with my guests, too." He turned to me again and gave me a wink.

"I understand you're working for your brother now."

"That's right," I said, not knowing what else to say.

"You should be out helping him now."

"He ain't workin'."

"He didn't go out tonight?"

"Him and George Hite went off somewheres."

He laughed again. I didn't like it. "He's working, all right," he said. "He'd better be. I like returns on my investments. But he's a good, ambitious boy. There's really nothing to worry about there."

I wondered what he meant, but he waved his hand at the girl. "Bring the kids what they want," he told her and she went away. I figured Johnny must of borrowed some money from him, but I didn't know why. He was a soldier and could of gone to the bank. Except he was a Lust, I thought, and drank some more of my beer. It was kind of yeasty. The girl brought two more glasses then.

Mr. Beazly turned to Stella again. "I have parties occasionally in the evening. I'd like you to come."

"Some night when Johnny isn't busy," she said.

"Of course," he said and got up to go. He winked at me again and said "Have a good time," and then turned away. I didn't even look at him, although it was nice of him to buy us some beer. I figured I knew why people said he was pretty shrewd. He said one thing when you could tell he meant something else. I wished Johnny hadn't got mixed up with him, either. Now there was bound to be trouble, sooner or later, the way people talked. I saw Stella look after him as he walked away, and I had a funny feeling inside. I didn't like it.

Pretty soon, she looked at her watch. "It's almost twelve," she said. "Johnny should be home. Maybe we'd better go." She didn't sound too anxious, but she took a sip of beer Red Beazly bought us and then got up.

"All right," I said, and we left. I didn't even taste the beer he bought me. All the way home Stella seemed to be thinking. When we got there, Johnny wasn't home, but she went in the bedroom and shut the door. I listened to Pa snore for a minute and heard Ma say something in her sleep, it was so quiet, and then I went and closed their door and went to sleep on the couch. I didn't even undress all the way. I was still thinking about Red Beazly and Johnny, and I guess I forgot.

Chapter 13

Johnny woke me when he came in, letting the door slam as he felt around for the string to the light. As he pulled it, I sat up on the couch, glad I had left my pants on.

"You should be asleep, kid," he said as he saw me.

"I was. You woke me."

"I didn't mean to." He paused a minute, like he didn't know what to say, and lit a cigarette. He was standing under the light and I could see his hand shake a little as he held the match. Then he asked, "How was the movie?"

"All right."

"Stella like it?"

"I guess. She acted like she did."

"Didn't she say? Was she mad or anything?"

"Not that I know of."

He walked over to the couch. "Well, what's eatin' you then? You act like you're sore or somethin'. I told you I didn't mean to wake you."

"Ma gave me hell before we went out."

He grinned. "What's so unusual about that?"

"She says I should stay away from Stella."

He laughed again. "Well, what the hell? Don't let that bother you. Sometimes I think Ma's got a dirty mind. I said it was okay, didn't I?"

I let that slide because I thought it was Johnny's way of showing it was silly and he didn't mean it. Besides, I had more important things to think about.

"We stopped at Red Beazly's on the way home."

"You what?" He sounded mad all of a sudden.

"We stopped at Red Beazly's. Stella wanted some fun."

"You stay away from that place. And keep Stella away. That's a hell of a place for kids. I thought you knew better." He calmed down then. "Red see you?" He asked as though he really didn't care, but I could see that he did.

"He came over and bought us a beer."

"What did he have to say?" He flicked ashes on the floor and then pulled a chair over and sat down.

"He asked Stella to dance."

"Did she?" He snapped it out real quick. I shouldn't of said it.

"No. Then he talked about you. Knew all about the junkyard. Said you wanted to get ahead. Then he said somethin' about a return on an investment."

Johnny laughed, but it didn't sound as though he meant it. "Hell, is that all?"

"Yeah. Then we come home."

Johnny pulled his chair a little closer and then leaned forward like he wanted to talk. "Look, Bobby. You're a nice kid, an' so is Stella. I wouldn't of married her if she wasn't. An' places like that are no good for either one of you. So don't go there again." He sounded serious but not mad or anything anymore.

"Not even if Stella wants to?"

"No. It's a good place to stay away from."

"Okay, if that's the way you want it. Myself, I don't care. I don't think Stella really does, either. She just wanted to get out, an' it was someplace to go."

"She'll get over that. She's still just a kid," he said, kind of relieved.

"Yeah," I said, and then looked away. "Johnny, what's this investment business he was talking about?"

"He loaned me some money. Where'd you think I got the dough for those tools and stuff I bought?"

"I figured that. Why did you go to him, though? You know how people talk. You should of tried the bank."

He gave another one of his short, sudden laughs. He knew I knew the answer to that. Then he looked at the bedroom door. It was closed, and you couldn't see any light through the crack. "What time did Stella go to bed?"

"I don't know . . . an hour ago at least."

He started to unbutton his shirt, one of his army ones, slowly, like he was in no hurry. For a second I could almost see Stella in there, lying across the bed, waiting for him. And sure as anything, he was going to spoil things. He didn't know how lucky he was.

"Johnny?"

"What kid?" He looked at me again, standing there with his shirt half-opened and the hair showing through. He was breathing heavily, like he was nervous or something.

"Johnny, what's going on? I got a right to know." I stood up, facing him, a few feet away, and I tried to keep my voice low.

He laughed again. "Hell, you know as much about it as I do."

"No, I don't. I don't know anythin' about it. Red Beazly as much as told me that."

"What did he say?" He just stood there a minute with his hands holding his shirt open.

"It wasn't what he said." I looked away, feeling that he was as scared, down underneath, as I was, and I didn't want to see it. "Johnny, what kind of crooked deal is goin' on?"

"Okay, kid, you're askin' for it." His voice was low and mean- sounding again. "You may as well sit down."

"I don't need to sit down."

"Have it your own way." He dropped his cigarette on the floor and stepped on it. "Kid, we're heistin' cars."

I sat down and looked up at him. "You mean all those out in the pasture?"

He laughed. "Well, no. You think we're that stupid? It's foolproof, I tell you. We can't miss."

"Yeah, like that hardware store business. Till the sheriff comes. Then you find out how foolproof it is."

"That was kid stuff. Do I have to draw you a picture?"

"Yeah." I felt kind of sick inside all of a sudden.

"We got all those nice junk cars out in the pasture, all bought an' paid for legally. An' each one has a nice title, made out to us." He grinned at me.

"So What?" I didn't get it, and anyway I didn't know what to say. It didn't make any difference. There wasn't anything I could say.

"We go out and pick up a car, same make an' model as one we got, an' all it takes then is a little number work on the block an' a new paint job, an' we're all set. We deliver 'em to a guy Red Beazly knows in Toledo an' get a nice wad of green money for our trouble. Just like that."

"Just like that." I kept looking at him.

"Yeah."

"An' you know how it's goin' to wind up."

"Nothin's goin' to upset it."

"Unless . . ."

"Unless what?"

"Nothin', Johnny. It's just that it's no good. In the first place it's crooked an' you can't get away with it. Sooner or later somebody's goin' to tell the sheriff."

Johnny laughed again. "Not a chance. Everybody who knows about it is in on it." He looked at me. "That includes you, too, kid, if you've got any ideas."

"I ain't got any ideas."

"You better not have." He started to unbutton his shirt again, and looked down at me. "Now you know. An' you'd better keep your mouth shut about it. You're in it as deep as the rest of us. You been workin' for us. An' you're a Lust. You don't have a chance." He laughed again. "Not unless you make your own chances, workin' with us." As he took his shirt off, he turned away.

"Johnny, don't get me wrong. It's not that I'm sore or anythin', but you got to get out of this mess."

"I know what I'm doin'."

"As far as you're concerned, maybe, but what about the rest? What about Ma'n Pa'n Stella? What you goin' to do when they find out?"

"If you keep your mouth shut, they're not goin' to."

"You can't keep it hid forever. They're not that dumb."

"Maybe by the time they find out they'll be so used to livin'good that they'll like the idea."

"You know better than that."

"Do I?" He turned to me again. "Well in that case, I don't give a good Goddamn what they think. This is my chance and nobody's goin' to spoil it. Nobody. Hear me? Nobody." His voice was low, but it was so strong that he might as well of yelled.

"Johnny, why don't you get out now, while you still can? If you do, nobody'll know."

"Don't be a sap."

"You could farm. This place would pay, an' there's money in farmin' now if you go at it right."

"Grub out my life on forty acres?"

"No, I mean it. Or get a job. Go back to Boston, like Stella said, an' get a job."

"Shut up! It's none of your Goddamned business." He yelled at me, and I got mad. I didn't want to, but I did.

"The hell it ain't," I told him. "I'm in it up to my neck now, like you said, an' I don't like it." I stood up facing him. "You don't care about anybody but yourself. You never did."

"I know what I'm doin', an' you or nobody else is goin' to stop me. So shut up." He stepped toward me.

"I got plenty more to say. An' I'm goin' to say it."

I saw it coming then, one of the short, choppy punches that he used to practice out in the barn when he was a kid, and I ducked, but his fist grazed my jaw and I felt a sudden sting and I remembered the ring he wore. I must of slipped and I fell back on the couch. He stood there looking down at me; his fists were still clenched and he was breathing hard.

"You asked for it. You want to learn the hard way, I'm just the guy who can teach you."

"Johnny!"

I don't know how long Stella'd been there, but she was standing in the doorway, wearing a thin nightgown that you could see through with the light behind her. She looked scared. I started to get up, but Johnny didn't even look at me. He turned slowly to look at Stella. His fists were still clenched.

"I suppose you know all about it now, too."

"I haven't been eavesdropping, if that's what you mean."

"It's a pretty fancy name, ain't it, for sneakin' around."

"Johnny, what's got into you? I never saw you like this before."

"You didn't know me as well as you thought, that's all. I know what I'm doin' an' I don't want other people buttin' in. If you didn't know that before, it's about time you found it out."

"That's not what I meant."

"You mean I'm a crook then."

"I didn't mean that either. But if . . ."

"Your Goddamn right I'm a crook if it means lookin' out for yourself and gettin' what's comin' to you."

"Johnny, I'm not going to stand for this much longer."

"You'll stand for it as long as I want you to."

"You had no right to hit Bobby."

Johnny acted like he'd forgotten I was there, and he didn't pay any attention to me. "That's nothin' compared to what anybody who gets in my way'll get. I promised you diamonds, and I'm goin' to get 'em the best way I know how."

"That was just talk, Johnny."

"You seemed to eat it up in that cheap restaurant I took you out of in Boston. You're just like the rest of 'em around here. Leave you be an' you'd rot an' love it. But I'm not made that way."

"Johnny, I . . . Oh, what's the use?" She turned suddenly and ran into the bedroom, slamming the door behind her. For a second I thought I heard her sob, and then Johnny turned to me. His lips were tight together and his face was shite.

"There's a thirty-nine Plymouth out in the barn. You go to work on it tomorrow morning. George Hite'll be in to show you what to do." His voice sounded tired all of a sudden, and he turned away, looked at the bedroom door for a minute, and then went in. He closed the door quietly, and I heard him say something to Stella. I couldn't hear her answer. I don't even know if she did.

My face still stung, and I brushed it with my fist. The blood had already begun to harden, and little pieces of it stuck to my hand. I looked at it for a minute and then laid down on the couch. After a while I got up and put out the light. I could hear them talking in the bedroom as I laid down again, but I couldn't understand the words. Pretty soon they quit, and I closed my eyes, but I was too nervous to sleep, and I wondered what I was going to do, especially in the morning. If I went to work on that car like Johnny told me to, I was sunk. And if I didn't, like he said, maybe I was sunk anyway, 'cause there were no jobs in town, and I heard they were moving the machinery out of the box factory.

I didn't want to think about it, but I couldn't help it. Every time I closed my eyes I saw Johnny swinging and I saw the car that they stole and I saw the sheriff. I thought about turning on the light and looking at the catalog, but that wouldn't help. It was the wishing book, Pa said, and it would make me feel like Johnny did about things. Sometimes I almost did anyway 'cause they made you think things was so easy. It was as bad as the movies.

I got to thinking of Stella, then, how she was in the movies and at Beazly's, like a kid, taking it all in, not knowing it was lies like so much that people tell you, and then I remembered her standing in the doorway, looking little and scared in her thin nightgown and I got to thinking how it would be if I was Johnny. But I wasn't and I tried to put the ideas out of my mind because they were no good. That was no use either, so finally I thought about her coming to me afraid and how I would help her. But I knew that I was scared, too, and I didn't know what to do. It was a long time before I could get to sleep, and all the time I was remembering about the last time Johnny got mixed up in actually stealing stuff. That time it was a car, too. You'd think he would learn. I thought about it for quite a while, trying to figure it all out. Now I knew he meant what he said.

Chapter 14

After Johnny got in trouble when he was sixteen, him and a town kid stealing guns and a tent from the hardware store and hiding them in our barn, he was pretty quiet for a long time, staying home in the evening like the judge said he had to, and even going back to school for a while til he kind of gradually quit going again. Then one day he came home and said he had a job and wasn't going back to school anymore. I guess the teachers were just as glad, 'cause none of them ever reported him. He was old enough to quit anyway, Pa said, and I guess Ma agreed with him.

Johnny's first job was working in a gas station down the road a few miles, and he really put in a lot of time, about twelve hours every day, for ten dollars a week. A lot of the time he was there alone, and I used to walk down once in a while to sit around with him. He'd give me candy and pop and stuff that they sold there. I didn't like to take it without paying for it, but Johnny said it was all right. It was part of his pay. Once or twice when I was there he forgot to put money from grease jobs in the cash register till I reminded him.

One thing, though, every week he gave Ma five dollars, even if she did say she didn't want it, he should save it. But she took it anyway, mostly 'cause Pa was only working now and then. Johnny used to buy stuff for all of us, too, whenever he could. Johnny never was stingy. When I was promoted in school, he bought all my books, new ones, too, 'cause he said second-hand ones weren't good enough, they were always all scribbled up when you got them.

He changed jobs kind of often, though, for the next three or four years, working in a couple of other gas stations and a garage, and for a while in the poolroom in town, but he never told Ma and Pa about that. Every time he quit, he said it was 'cause he wasn't getting enough money, but a couple of times he got in fights with the guy he was working for. The customers all liked Johnny, though, wherever he worked. They said he was full of fun.

Once, then, not long after the beginning of the war, when I got off the school bus and come in the house, nobody was around. Pa was working off and on for a man building a barn, and I figured he was working, but I wondered where Ma was. She never went anyplace 'cept to church and once in a while into town, when Pa's old car was working.

It was cold in the house, and the fire was out in the kitchen stove, so I figured she'd been gone for a long time. She never let the fire go out if she could help it. I got wood and some coal and papers and stuff from the woodshed and laid a fire. I threw a little coal oil in, and it started right off. I figured Ma could start supper right off then when she got home. I was pretty hungry.

While I was standing in front of the stove to warm up a little, I remembered then that Johnny hadn't come in yet by the time I went to school that morning. I didn't think much of it then because quite a few times Johnny'd come sneaking in at four or five o'clock in the morning, as quiet as he could so's he wouldn't wake Pa and Ma. He'd been doing that ever since the judge let him off of probation.

Still, I figured, Ma couldn't of gone looking for him 'cause she didn't have any way of getting into town, and besides, she wouldn't know where to look for him. And she didn't seem worried or anything that morning anyway, before I left.

It was getting pretty late, and I ate a big chuink of Ma's bread and jelly, but still nobody came. It was getting dark already, and I was getting kind of worried when I heard a car pull up into the lane. I wondered whose it was, Pa's wasn't working anymore and he rode to work with some men, so I looked out the window. It was a black one with a big silver shield on the door.

I was too scared to go over near the door, and when it opened I felt like running into the other room. But I just stood there, and Ma came into the room. Pa was behind her, and then Johnny, and then another man I never saw before. He was fat and wearing an overcoat and a hat the way I'd seen cops do in the movies. Nobody said anything at first, and then I ran over to Ma. I was almost as tall as her then, and I felt a little silly in front of everybody, but I was scared.

"Ma, where have you been?" She looked like she'd been crying or something. "What's the matter, Ma? I been worried."

"I'm sorry, son. I should of left a note or something, but I ran off. I just never thought." She put her hand on my arm and then took it off right away. "I'll fix you some supper," she said.

"It's okay, Ma. I ain't very hungry. I ate some bread and jelly a little while ago."

I noticed then that everybody was standing around with their coats still on. Nobody said anything, not even Johnny. All I could think of was trouble, but I didn't know what kind, and I was too scared to ask. I just stood there like the rest of them.

Then the fat man started to talk. He was looking at Johnny. "Well, Lust, you get yourself a good night's sleep and I'll be down to pick you up early in the morning. We've got to be at the recruiting station by eight o'clock."

"Don't worry. I'll be here," Johnny said, kind of mean.

"You'd better be," the man said, and then went to the door. He said, "Goodnight, everybody," just as he went out, but nobody answered. We all just stood there like we was.

Then I spoke up, like a fool. "Johnny, gou goin' to the army? What did the man mean, recruitin' station? You and him goin' together? I didn't even know you was thinkin' of goin' to the war." I was glad all of a sudden that that's what it was. I always thought in school it would really be something to be in a war. Around a battle field you could pick up drums and things that were laying around.

"Yeah, I'm goin' to the army, all right. I wasn't plannin' on it, but it looks like I'm goin'," Johnny said, not sounding like himself at all. I could hardly hear him, and I figured he was probably nervous or something like you'd get when you knew that you're going.

"That's really somethin', Johnny. I sure wish I was old enough to go along."

"Don't get me wrong, kid. It ain't my idea of a good time. They wouldn't get me in the army on a bet without a cop behind me to make me go."

"You mean you got to go, Johnny? You ain't goin' 'cause you want to?"

"You think I'm a fool? The judge gave me my choice--to to the army, or go to jail. It's pro'bly better than jail." He took off his coat and started to whistle. I looked at Ma. She was taking hers off. Pa just stood there. I didn't know what to make of it, so I turned to Ma.

"Ma, what's the matter? Is Johnny in trouble?"

"It's Johnny's affair. You better ask him." She started to get things down from the cupboard. I looked at Johnny again.

"What's the matter, Johnny? What's the judge got to do about it?"

"It's a long story, kid. It all boils down to the fact that I'm no good. The judge figures the army can straighten me out. More'n likely, he figures it's cheaper than havin' a trial and sendin' me to jail. Besides I might be out of the way permanently this way, if I happen to get knocked off."

Ma spoke up then, sounding kind of mad. "It wasn't that way at all. He was givin' you another chance, an' you got to do right this time, whatever the army wants you to do. He was a nice old man, tryin' to help you."

"If he wanted to help me, he could of turned me loose."

"An have you turn around an . . ." Ma turned away and started rattling pans in the cupboard. She said something else, but I couldn't tell what. I was kind of mixed up inside, and I just stood there looking at Johnny.

"Well, don't you want to hear the rest of it, about your big brother gettin' picked up an' havin' to spend the night in the tank, with a couple of drunks heavin' all over the place?"

"Johnny!" Ma yelled out real sudden, without turning around.

"What's the matter? Don't you want me to talk about it? Don 't you want to listen so's you can gloat over the wages of sin an' spendin' the night in the clink an' gettin' sent to the army?" Johnny turned around and was yelling at Ma.

Pa spoke up then. "I ain't beat you in a long time, not since the last time you got in a mess, but by God . . ."

Johnny didn't give him a chance to finish. "Yeah, the last time. The last time I got caught, I was a fool then, like last night, but not any more. It don't take me too many times to catch on. Twice is enough." He pulled a chair away from the table. "Let's all sit down and have a party. Tomorrow I go off to be a hero. A tin hero in a brown suit instead of a jailbird in stripes."

"Johnny, shut up!" I yelled at him all of a sudden. "Don't you even talk about it," I went on then, kind of scared at yelling out like that. "I don't care what happened."

"You, too, huh? It's too nasty to talk about, huh?" Johnny didn't talk so loud then, though, like he was tired of talking.

Ma had some eggs and bacon frying then in two of her frying pans, and all you could hear was the sizzle of hot grease for a couple of minutes. It started to smell good. I'd forgotten I was still hungry. I was going to sit down, but then I went over to the cupboard where Ma was getting out dishes.

"I'll set the table, Ma," I said, mostly to have something to do.

"You go sit down. It won't take but a minute."

I went back to the table again. Johnny was sitting there with his head in his hands. Pa had picked up a paper and was looking at it. He didn't seem to be reading, though, just looking at it. I tried not to look at them as I went to sit down. Nobody said anything as Ma set the table.

Pa folded up the paper and put it in his pocket as Ma dished up the bacon and eggs. With some of her bread sliced up on a plate, it sure looked good to me, and I went ahead and ate like a horse until I noticed nobody else was eating much. Then I slowed down, but I kept on eating 'cause I didn't have to talk or even think about what was going on. But even the bread didn't taste too good anymore.

Johnny got up from the table then and looked out the door. Ma watched him for a minute and then said, "You'd better sit down and finish your supper, son. Your eggs are gettin' cold." They were, too, because the grease around them looked hard.

"I don't need to, Ma," Johnny said. "The army'll fatten me up. Like you do young bulls before you stick a knife in their throats."

"Don't talk foolishness. It ain't like it was forever. An' lots of the boys are goin' now. I don't hold with fightin', but sometimes you got to." The way she looked at Johnny you could see how she liked him. "Want me to fry you some more eggs, Johnny? These are too cold to eat."

"I said I don't want any. Leave me alone." Johnny kept staring out the window. I wondered what he could see, it was so dark. Maybe a light or two down the hill would be all.

I started to think how lucky he was, going to the army, even if he didn't think so. Except for the killing part, it ought to be fun, wearing a uniform and drilling and having a lot of guys around just like you to knock around with, going to shows and stuff. And getting to go to places most people only read of in books.

I got to thinking so hard I didn't even notice Johnny come back and sit down till he pulled his chair over closer to Ma's. Pa didn't even move. He was already just about asleep in his chair.

"I guess I sure made a mess of things, didn't I, Ma?" Johnny said then after a while.

"We all make a mess once in a while," Ma said. "You just got to try an' do right from now on is all."

"But who says what's right? What did I do wrong?"

"You took somebody else's car out for a ride. You can't do that, son. You ought to know better than that."

"Some old pot belly who runs a store. What right's he got to it, any more than me? Christ, I work harder than him. And I needed it for a date."

"Don't talk that way, son," Ma said, kind of sharp.

"I can't help it. It's the truth, ain't it? Who makes all these don'ts? The ones who want to keep things all for themselves. They must think we're a bunch of saps. How did they get it themselves? Look at old man

Graves. The richest guy in town. How'd he get that way? By lettin' people keep what they worked for? Hell, he'd of taken the farm if Pa hadn't sold everythin' to pay him off."

"Johnny, I don't know what to say," Ma said, rubbing her eyes on the sleeve of her good dress. "It ain't right to talk that way about things. It's God's will, remember."

"Sure. Old Man Graves is an elder in the church. But what did God ever do for us?" He looked over at me then. "Bobby, why don't you go to bed? You're too young to know all this. But hell, I knew it when I was your age, I guess."

I let my hand drop and didn't say anything. I'd kind of thought like that myself, even if I never said anything. But what could you do? Except work and try to keep out of trouble, I thought to myself. That's all you could do.

Ma's face was all red, and she was biting her lip. I thought she was going to cry. I'd never seen her cry, and I didn't know what I would do. I wanted to run and I wanted to listen to Johnny and yell that he was right. But I just sat there, trying not to look at Ma.

"Good God, Ma," Johnny said. "There's nothin' to cry about. When I get out of the army, I'll be all right. I'll show 'em, an' take care of you. I'll make more money than old Graves, only not the same way. I don't want to throw people out in the street."

"Johnny, money don't matter. It's the way that you live."

"Money decides the way you can live. An' I'm goin' to get my share an' more, as much as I can."

120

"You're just talkin', Johnny. You don't mean all that.,"

"I mean it more'n I ever meant anythin'. You'll see."

"Don't talk any more." Ma got up and looked down at him. "Maybe the army'll teach you better. God knows I can't. You're just like your Pa." She sounded real tired. "I tried, Johnny. To teach you right. But I guess I didn't try hard enough or somethin'." She started to pick up the dishes. "Just try to live right. That's all that makes any difference."

Johnny got up then. "Don't worry, Ma. I'll keep my mouth shut in the army an' do what I'm told. They can do too much to a man if he don't. But you'll see when I get out."

Ma didn't say any more, but took the hot water from the stove over to the sink. Johnny went in the bedroom, and I heard his shoes drop on the floor. When Ma cleared the table off, I got my books to do my lessons, but I couldn't keep my mind on them. I was thinking with Johnny in the army things sure would be different.

And they were different, for almost four years, I was thinking as I laid on the couch. Things were so quiet it didn't seem possible now. Pa worked off and on, and I got a job after school and then quit when I got into the box factory, and Johnny came home on furlough a couple of times, looking fine in his uniform, and even got his name in the paper when he went across. Things would of been fine if Ma hadn't of got sick.

Ma started getting sick, right after Johnny went away, with pains in her side and back. She didn't tell Pa or me till one morning when she couldn't get up.

We got the doctor, and he couldn't find anything wrong, so he gave her some pills. She slept a lot after that, and after a couple of weeks, she got up again. She still got the pains, but after a long time they went away. I asked the doctor once what it was, and he said nerves. Women get that way sometimes when they had a boy in the army. I figured right then it was more than just that, but I never said anything about it. Ma didn't have the pains now for more than a year, and now he was home again, getting ready to steal. And I was in it, too, and I laid awake for hours trying to figure out what I could do. Finally I fell asleep, and I dreamed I was in jail.

Chapter 15

Once I got to sleep, I woke up a couple of times scared like something was ready to happen, and the last time, I got up and got dressed. It was getting daylight, but nobody was up. I figured out what I was going to do. Before Johnny got up, I'd take the truck and go looking for a job. And I wouldn't come home till I found one, no matter how long it would take me. There had to be some place in town a guy could find a job if he was willing to work.

I was cutting some bread to fix myself something to eat when Ma came in the kitchen. She was all dressed already.

"You're up pretty early, Bobby. What's the matter, can't you sleep?"

"I slept all right, but I figured I'd get up early. I'm goin' in town an' look for a job." I went over to get the butter out of the icebox so's she wouldn't see the cut on my face.

"What's the matter, ain't you and Johnny gettin' along the way you ought to?"

"It ain't that, Ma. I'm just gettin' tired of workin' in the barn all the time."

"It's better workin' around home. That's where your brother should be, too, 'stead of chasin' around all the time."

"He will be, Ma, now he's gettin' things started," I said, spreading butter on my bread and getting a glass of water.

"I hope so, son." Then she looked at the bread I'd cut for myself. "That's no breakfast, son. I'll fry you some eggs," Ma said as I sat down at the table. "Wait till I put the coffee on."

That's what I was afraid of, with her getting up. It would take too much time, and then Johnny'd be up. "It's okay, Ma," I said. "I want to get an early start. That's the best time to look for a job, early in the morning." I started to eat.

"You can't do it on an empty stomach," Ma said, and then came over close to me. "Bobby, what happened to your face?"

"What's the matter with it?" I said, as calm as I could. "Is there anything wrong with it, Ma?" I took a bite of bread.

"There's a cut on your chin. It's been bleedin'." Ma came over closer to look, and I felt it with my hand.

"I must of cut it out in the barn," I said, chewing my bread like it was nothing.

"You better let me put somethin' on it."

"It's okay, Ma," I said. "It's only a scratch anyway."

"You didn't have it at supper last night," Ma said after a minute. "An' I heard some noise out here last night."

"Maybe I cut it in my sleep, Ma. I never noticed it."

"It don't look like that kind of cut, son." She bent over and looked at it for a minute.

"Have you and your brother been fightin'?" she asked, straightening up.

"No, Ma. What would we be fightin' about? We get along pretty well, Johnny an' me, as well as anybody, I guess."

"Then what was the ruckus I heard in here last night?"

"I don't know, Ma, honest I don't." I took a drink of water just to have something to do. I didn't want to lie to Ma, but what else could I do? I just hoped she'd quit asking questions and let me go before Johnny got up. he'd probably start saying things and I'd get mad and Ma would find out all about everything. But I couldn't rush Ma, I had to go easy.

"An' now you want to go get a job in town. You don't want to work around here helpin' Johnny anymore. Son, what's goin' on between you two.? Was it anything about you goin' out with Stella? I got a right to know. I'm your mother."

"Nothin's goin' on, Ma, honest. I'd tell you if there was, but there ain't nothin' to tell. I'm just tired of workin' around here, an' besides, I ain't makin' any money at all."

"You got to build up the business first. You and Johnny together."

"An' George Hite, Ma. Don't forget George Hite. He's Johnny's partner, not me." I said it kind of nasty without thinking.

"Is that what the fight was about? George Hite? What's he got to do with it? What's the two of 'em doin'?"

"Nothin', Ma. There wasn't any fight," I kind of yelled at her.

You can't lie to me, son. I ain't very smart, I guess, but I know a lie when I hear one. Specially when it's my own son lyin'." She turned away and went back by the stove. I didn't say any more, but just sat there for a minute, not knowing what to do. Ma had a right to know all about it, and she was bound to find out sooner or later, but I couldn't tell her. I just had to keep on lying my head off.

I finished my bread and was drinking the water when Ma came over to the table again with a glass of milk.

"Here, son, drink this, at least. You got to have more than bread."

"Thanks, Ma," I said, though I really didn't want it. it was just something to take up more time, and all the while it was getting closer to the time Johnny got up. I started to drink the milk, but I was kind of full from the water. Ma just stood there looking at me, and as I finished the milk, Pa came into the room. I didn't even look at him. I jumped up and said, "Well, I got to be goin', Ma. I'll prob'ly be home by noon." I went outside before I had to say any more, and went down and got my truck.

The motor didn't start right off, but finally it caught hold. I let it warm up a minute and then drove up by the house. I looked down at the gas gauge then, and the needle was jumping around right on the big E for empty. And I didn't have any money in my pocket. I'd put the change from the five dollars Johnny gave me on a shelf in the kitchen. I was scared he'd be up, but I had to go and get it. It was all the money I had, or for that matter, all I was likely to get for a while unless Johnny paid me back.

I turned the motor off to save gas and went in the house. Just Pa and Ma were in the kitchen, and Ma was frying eggs. She didn't hear me, and Pa didn't even look up when I got the money. There was a dollar bill and some change. I put it in my pocket and was just getting ready to go when Johnny came in.

"I thought I heard the truck," he said, looking at me. "Where do you think you're goin' this mornin', kid?"

"I got to go into town. I've got things I want to do."

"You got plenty to do in the barn. George Hite's comin' in this mornin' to show you what to do."

I glanced over at Ma. She was just standing there, taking it all in. I figured there was only one thing to do, so I looked back at Johnny. He was standing there, grinning at me, but I made up my mind I wasn't going to get mad, no matter what.

"I'm goin' to town to look for a job. I ain't cut out for the junk business," I said, looking him in the eye. "I made up my mind last night. So I got to use the truck."

"Hell, go ahead use it. It don't make any difference to me." He laughed at me then and turned to Ma. "It's a good thing you got one smart son, Ma. That one'll never take any prizes for brains." He turned around to me then. "Well, what you standin' around for? Go ahead and look for a job. I ain't beggin' for the chance to give you a break. Maybe you can get a job peddlin' papers or somethin'. Then when you get your belly full, come back. Maybe then you'll appreciate what I'm tryin' to do for you."

I just stood there looking at him. I didn't expect this.

"Go on, get goin'." Johnny said. "Get out. I got enough to think about without botherin' with you any more. Just remember what I told you last night, that's all."

I turned then and almost ran out the door to the truck. This time the motor started right off, and I headed for town.

After I got some gas, I wondered where I should start. There wasn't much in Titus except stores and gas stations and garages and a little factory that made furniture. Now that the box factory was closed, there sure wasn't much.

I tried the furniture factory first, and the man said they was full up. He took my name, though and gave me a form to fill out and bring in, and he said if he needed anybody, he'd let me know. Once in a while somebody would quit. Other than that there wasn't much chance. After I left there, I tried thre or four stores on Main Street and then the feed and grain store, but there was nothing doing. Two guys working in the feed store told me the best thing to do was get out of Titus. I figured that was the best idea, but I didn't know where.

There was no sense going around to other places, I figured, but I went anyway, till I got sick of asking and having them tell me "No." But I hated the idea of going back to the farm, like Johnny said, with my tail between my legs, and work with George Hite. Just just like Johnny said, I was in it anyhow, as deep as they were, and there wasn't much I could do about it now, especially with no job.

All the way back to the farm I kept trying to figure how I could make Johnny forget about stealing cars, but I couldn't. He'd made up his mind, and he was in it. The junk business wouldn't be bad, and I wouldn't mind it at all if they hadn't stole that car. First thing I knew, as I pulled into the lane, I was wishing they'd got caught while they were stealing it. Things would of been simpler.

I parked the truck by the side door and went into the house, wondering what to tell Johnny if he said anything. They were all sitting at the table, almost through eating, and nobody said anything to me. There was a place for me and I sat down. Johnny looked at me and winked, like it didn't make any difference. But I knew that it did.

After I started to eat, Johnny got up, wiping his mouth. He came around the table and stopped by me. "When you get through eatin', come out in the barn. You better change your clothes, though. We got plenty to do."

I didn't say anything, but kept on eating. Stella looked across at me kind of funny and I looked down at my plate. Johnny went on out without saying anymore. I guess he knew as well as I did there wasn't anything else I could do. I was in it, anyway, I told myself, I might as well get some of the gravy. But I couldn't really believe it. Sooner or later the sheriff would come.

After Johnny went out, Ma passed me more meat. "You're prob'ly pretty hungry, son. Better take more."

"I ain't too hungry, Ma. I stopped for some coffee."

"Did you find anything to do?" she asked after a minute.

"No. There ain't much doin' in town, I guess. Every place told me they was full. Guess I'll have to keep workin' for Johnny."

"Maybe it'll all work out for the best."

"Yeah, maybe," I said, but I didn't mean it. There was only one way I figured it could ever work out. But I couldn't tell Ma.

After I ate, I put on my overalls in the front room and went out to the barn. The big doors were closed, and the little door was hooked on the inside. I hammered on it for a minute, and then Johnny opened it, grinning.

"Hi, kid," he said. "You look like you're ready for business."

"I am," I said and went inside. Johnny hooked the door behind me. It sure was hot in there, but I fugured Johnny had reasons for keeping the place closed up.

The thirty-nine Plymouth was sitting in the center of the floor, in the part I'd cleaned up, and George Hite had the hood up and was hammering on the side of the motor. I went over and watched him for a minute, and then Johnny came over and stood by me, looking on.

"George'll show you what to do, kid. You work with him," Johnny said, and then yawned. "I'd better go up to the house and catch myself some sleep." He put his hand on my shoulder then. "Just don't make any mistakes. Remember that, an' everythin's goin' to be fine. There's nothing to be scared of unless you want to be scared. But we can't afford any mistakes."

"I'll be careful, Johnny," I said. "I ain't no fool."

"I know you ain't, kid, even if you act like one sometimes." He laughed for a minute. "Hook the door after
me, will you, kid? And don't let anybody nose around."

"I won't, Johnny," I said and followed him over to
the door. When I got back, George Hite was standing
up, wiping his hands on a rag. There was grease all
over his face.

"Well, you ready to go to work for a change?"

"I been workin' right along while you an' Johnny
been out chasin' around," I said, kind of mad. "Who
did all the work here in the barn?"

"Don't get cocky, kid. That part ain't important.
Now the work is really beginnin'."

"What am I supposed to do?"

"Hand me stuff for a while. We got to change the
numbers before anythin' else."

"Okay," I said. "Let's get to work." I tried to sound as
much like Johnny as I could.

Chapter 16

One thing I can say for George Hite, he really knew
cars, and he kept me so busy the next couple of days
that I didn't even get a chance to think. He was nasty
and kind of sarcastic most of the time, and I still didn't
like him, but when we got through, we had a good looking Plymouth. We'd changed the numbers on the block
and body, cleaned it up, and gave it a new paint job.
Johnny took it away as soon as the paint was dry. By
that time I had almost forgotten it was stolen and I was
kind of sorry to see it go. George Hite and me sat on
the bench outside the barn and watched Johnny drive
down the lane. The new green paint was shiny in the afternoon sun, and I was tired but I felt pretty good. As
long as I didn't let myself think. With George Hite
around and nothing to do except listen to him now that
the car was gone, it was pretty hard.

"There goes about five hundred bucks worth of car
as far as we're concerned, kid. Sure beats the Goddamn box factory, don't it?"

I didn't answer him, but looked over toward the
house, half- hoping I'd see Stella. I didn't see much of
her any more, and when I did, at supper mostly, she
didn't talk much.

Afterwards she'd help Ma with the dishes and then
go in her room. She'd shut the door, and Johnny would
sit and joke with Pa till Pa dozed in his chair. One
night he brought out a bottle and they poured me a
drink. Ma cried and I didn't take it. Pa and Johnny got
kind of drunk, and when Johnny went in the bedroom,

he talked pretty loud for a while. I went outside so I wouldn't have to listen.

I'd almost forgot George Hite sitting beside me until he stuck a pack of ciagrettes in front of my face.

"Here, have one, kid. Nobody's watchin'."

"I don't want one, George."

"Hell, go ahead. Your Ma won't see you."

"That's not the reason."

He took the pack away and lit one up. "That's the only reason for anythin'. You might get caught. Most of 'em are like you, though. They don't admit it. Me, I do." He laughed. "It's not what you do, it's what you get away with that counts. An' we got ourselves a sweet deal."

"Yeah," I said. I didn't mean it, but I hoped he'd shut up.

"As long as we look out for ourselves, that is."

"Don't you think we ought to sell a few parts once in a while?"

"We will. Give us time."

"People'll begin to wonder."

"We got to build up a stock. You don't want to be a parts man, do you, Bobby? It's a lot more work than goin' over these heaps, an' you take too much crap."

"I wouldn't mind."

"No money in it, kid. You stick with me. I'll teach you a real trade. Hell, there's nothing to worry about. You act like your old man sometimes. Keep on and you'll wind up like your Pa. That's what comes from bein' afraid."

I didn't say anything then because I saw Stella come out of the side door. She walked around the back of the house and down the path to the privy. Even from that distance you could tell she was pretty, with her dark hair, and slacks and one of her bright red sweaters on. I watched till I couldn't see her anymore. Then George Hite laughed.

"That's pretty nice, ain't it, kid? Johnny sure picked up somethin', there. She looks like she'd know how to please a man an' enjoy doin' it, too."

Out of the corner of my eye, I could see him watching me and grinning. I didn't know what to say.

"She's really put together, ain't she, Bobby? You ever think how it'd be to have somethin' like that around to climb onto whenever you wanted?"

I could feel my face getting hot, but I didn't say anything. I hoped he'd shut up and yet part of me wanted to listen. I looked away.

"Go ahead an' stare at the place, kid. Don't mind me."

"Shut up!"

He laughed at me. "You don't have to hide it, kid. Hell, there'd be somethin' wrong with a man didn't feel like that when he looked at her. Can't you picture yourself . . ?"

I got up and went into the barn, but I could still hear his voice in my ears, low and kind of sharp like a knife sliding into a ripe melon. He said something about a guy needing money to sport something like that, but I didn't pay any attention. I started to pick up the papers that we'd used to mask the windows and the chrome on the Plymouth, but after a minute or two I quit. I couldn't help thinking how it would be, and I kicked at the papers. There wasn't much else a guy could do.

Pretty soon I heard George Hite start to whistle some slow mournful song. He stuck his head inside the door. "Dream on, kid. An' clean the place up while you're at it. I'm goin' down an' have a drink with your old man." He pulled the door shut behind him. I waited till I was sure he was gone before I opened it again, and then I cleaned the grease off my hands with some straw and sand and old rags. I couldn't get the paint off, though, and it showed up bright green on my skin. The harder I rubbed, the brighter it seemed to get, so I quit. It was just like everything else. Fighting only made it hurt too.

It was hot and kind of damp in the barn, and the fresh, strong smell of paint made me feel kind of sick. There was a lot of other places I'd rather be than trying to get the place ready for the next job. There was a lot of things I'd rather be doing, too, and as I straightened up around, I thought about them, not on purpose, but just the way they came into my mind. In every one of them I had a lot of money and there was a girl looked like Stella. And I picked up papers and cleaned tools and the spray gun, without a nickel in my pocket, with George Hite probably telling Pa I was hot for my brother's wife. I felt like a fool, but I kept on thinking about things.

There was a tool crib that we'd made in a corner of the barn by fencing it off with boards and putting up a door. I was inside it putting tools away in some racks I'd made when I heard somebody come into the barn. I thought it was George Hite, come back to needle me some more, and I felt like hiding. As I turned around, I had a sudden wild hope that it was Stella. I went out and it was. She was standing inside the door, breathing hard, like she'd been running. I tried not to look at her bright colored sweater. It was pretty hard not to.

"Hi, Bobby."

"Hi."

"I couldn't stand it in the house any more. George Hite and Pa are in the kitchen."

"I don't blame you." I felt funny, like she could see into my mind. 'But this old barn is no place for a girl."

"Where is there a place?"

I knew what she meant, and I turned away. "I was cleanin' the place up, puttin' stuff in order," I told her just to say something.

"When is Johnny coming back?"

"I don't know...he went to Toledo." I shouldn't of said it, but I did, why, I don't know.

"Oh. Why didn't he say something to me about it?"

"Didn't he?" I said, bending over to pick up a scrap of paper.

"You know he didn't. Bobby, look at me."

I straightened up and looked, half afraid to, not knowing what she wanted or what I would do. I felt warm all over.

"What is it, Bobby? Is it something wrong with me?"

I shook my head, but she didn't pay any attention.

"Why doesn't he tell me things or take me places? Is he ashamed of me or doesn't he trust me or what? I married him because I loved him and that means some-

136

thing. At least I thought it did," she added. "Now I don't know what to think." She turned and looked out the door. Her shoulders were shaking a little. I watched her for a minute, not knowing what to say, and then she turned around again, just as suddenly.

"Have you got anything planned for tonight, Bobby?"

"Course not." I couldn't keep my eyes off her bright sweater. She must of known it. She couldn't help it.

"Like to help an old married woman kill time while her husband is out of town?"

"I . . . I wasn't sure what to say. But hell. Suddenly I felt strong and cocky. "Sure, Stella. I'll be glad to," I said. I was in everything else up to my neck. And like Johnny said, you got to make your own breaks.

"Okay, Bobby," she said. "We'll really paint up the town." She smiled, but it seemed kind of forced, and then turned to go. I stood in the doorway and watched her walk back up to the house, still feeling warm all over. After she went in, I remembered I didn't have any money. And then the warm feeling went away and I felt like a bastard again. This time I had to force myself to think about her and how it would be.

Chapter 17

We sat in Red Beazly's and I saw it happen right before my eyes. It was after midnight, and we'd spent the six dollars I'd got for some old batteries I hauled to the junkman in town and we'd each had five or six drinks and I was sleepy. I felt a little silly, and I kept making Stella laugh, imitating people around town, but somehow the edge had worn off and I was ready to go home. It was spoiled when Stella wanted to dance and I got scared and said no. I couldn't stand to have people see me hold her, but I couldn't say that, and then it was too late. Red Beazly sat down at our table.

"Hi, kids. Having a good time, I hope." He winked at me and then turned to Stella, leaving me to look at the bright yellow back of his sport coat. "Where's that big handsome husband of yours tonight?"

"You should know," she told him. "I understand that you're pretty well acquainted with my husband's affairs." She didn't sound mad or anything when she said it, and she kind of giggled as she sipped at her drink.

"I've been expecting you back. In fact, I've been watching for you."

"Are you always so concerned about your customers?"

"Always...when they permit me to be. Of course, I never intrude."

The hell you don't, I wanted to say, but I didn't have the nerve. There was something going on, but I didn't know what, and I was getting sore at both of them. I figured I'd better take Stella home, and I took a drink and then coughed pretty loud. They didn't pay any attention. Beazly said something I didn't hear and then Stella laughed. I knew I'd better get her out of there. Johnny would be mad enough as it was. I leaned forward across the table so I could see Stella.

"We better get home, Stella. It's gettin' kind of late," I said, interrupting whatever it was Beazly was saying. He turned slowly to look at me, raising his eyebrows like he'd been practicing doing it.

"You shouldn't be in any hurry, kid. You've been working hard and deserve a little fun. And you don't mind if Stella has a good time, do you?"

"We better go home," I said again, kind of mad. It was none of his business.

"Let's not go yet, Bobby." Stella smiled at me. "It's so seldom we get out."

"It's after midnight an' Johnny's goin' to be mad as it is. Besides," I added and then stopped.

"Besides what, Bobby?" Stella asked.

"Besides you remember you're a married woman." I hated to say it because I'd been trying so hard to forget it, but she asked for it, and I couldn't think of anything else. I looked at Beazly, waiting for him to say something. He raised his eyebrows again.

"A puritan," he said, and Stella giggled. It made me sore, and I got up, facing both of them.

"Look, it's time to go home an' I'm goin'. You comin' along, Stella?" I made it sound as much like Johnny as I could, but I knew it didn't have that meanness and not caring that he could put into things. Stella quit giggling, though, and looked up at me quickly. Then she looked at Beazly.

"Why don't you let the boy go home if he's so set on it, Stella? After all, just because he's leaving is no reason for you to."

I felt like slugging him and I knew Johnny would of, but I made like I didn't hear it and waited for Stella to say something. She looked back at me.

"Don't be in such a rush, Bobby." She smiled again, and probably I would of sat down, but I was still mad. I didn't say anything, just stood there looking at them.

"Besides, I did want to dance and you wouldn't dance with me, Bobby. I'm having fun. Don't spoil it."

"Johnny didn't want us comin' here. If we have sense enough to go home, maybe he won't be too sore."

She laughed at me then. "Everybody's afraid of Johnny! Well, I'm not and it's about time he finds it out." She drank the rest of her drink while I stood there feeling like a fool and then she put the glass down on the table. "Take your old truck and go home. I'm going to stay and have some fun." She looked back at Beazly, who was sitting there smiling and .pa taking it all in. "You have some nice records on your jukebox, Mr. Beazly. I admire your taste."

"Okay," I said as calmly as I could and walked away, trying not to seem in a hurry as I went to the door. It seemed like everybody in the place was watching me and I didn't look back.

After I sat out in the truck for a while, where the noise wasn't so loud and it was cool and a nice soft breeze was blowing through the open windows, I calmed down considerably, and I thought about going back in. Then when I thought how they'd look at me or laugh or maybe be dancing, I felt like a fool again, and even in the truck with nobody looking at me I felt warm all over. I figured what then hell then and started home. But I felt pretty lousy because no matter what happened, it would be all my fault. If I'd had any sense, none of this would of happened, but I never did the right thing anyhow, and if Johnny found out, there would really be hell to pay. Well, I wouldn't tell him, I figured, and then felt some better. But not much.

I half-expected to find Ma still up, fretting and praying and ready to bawl me out, but the place was dark. I left the truck beside the house because there wasn't room for it in the barn any more, and went inside. It was no use going to bed, though, 'cause I knew I'd be worrying about Stella and everything, so I lit the light and sat there thumbing through the catalog. I'd have to make it up to Johnny somehow, but I didn't know how.

I guess I must of dozed off then because the next thing I knew somebody was shaking me by the shoulder. At first I thought it was Pa but then I saw it was Stella. She seemed excited, but not mad or anything. I pretended I was harder waking up than I really was.

"Bobby, wake up. I want to talk to you."

"I'm awake," I told her finally.

She stepped back then and looked down at me. Her face was in the shadow. "I'm sorry for the way I acted tonight," she said. "I don't know what made me stay."

I wasn't sure whether she meant it or not. "It's all right," I said. "Don't worry about it." Then: "What time is it?" I wanted to ask her if Red Beazly brought her home, but I didn't want to even think about that.

"After three," she said. "Johnny isn't home yet, is he?"

I shook my head. "I don't think so."

"You won't tell him...that I stayed, that is?"

"No," I said. I didn't want to think about it, and I wished she'd go away. She looked at me for a minute. "Thanks, Bobby," she said in a low voice. "I won't forget it."

"It's okay," I said and then she went into her room.

She walked as though she hadn't had anything at all to drink. I wanted to ask her what she'd been doing, and I felt kind of excited, but I didn't dare. Instead I took off my clothes and pulled the light string. As I went back to the couch, I noticed that her door was standing open ten inches or so and I could see her shadow as she moved around inside the room. I laid down on the couch, still watching her shadow. She was humming to herself, loud enough so I could hear. I'd never heard her hum before. I was excited and I knew I was a crazy fool, and the bedsprings made a singing noise as she laid down with the lights still on and I had to look away. I was shaking. Finally, after what seemed like a year, she turned out the light.

Chapter 18

All the next morning while I was working I couldn't get my mind off Stella. Not about her staying with Red Beazly so much, although that was part of it, but mostly about her humming and moving around inside the room so's her shadow came so close to me and then moved away just out of reach. I was a fool, I knew, but I couldn't help it. I kept telling myself she was no good, staying at Red Beazly's like that while Johnny was out, but that didn't help any, because I kept thinking I didn't blame her, the way Johnny acted. I only wished I was a little bigger or a little smarter or that Johnny wasn't my brother. But things weren't that way.

We were working over a forty-one Ford that Johnny'd brought in the night before, and while we were getting set up, George Hite kept looking at me kind of funny, like he knew something was up. I tried not to pay any attention, but it was pretty hard not to. It was getting on my nerves. Finally, when I was holding the light so's George could see under the hood, I bumped a hammer that was laying on the fender. It slipped down and must of hit George on the hand. He jumped up, looking pretty mad.

"I didn't mean it, George," I said. "I just bumped it an' it fell."

"Damn right it fell, right on my hand. You're goin' to have to quit your moonin' durin' workin' hours. Well, kid, this is tricky enough as it is. You want to ruin this whole numbers job an' have us all wind up in the can?" He didn't sound so mad anymore, but he wiped his hands on a rag and looked at his fingers under the light.

"Maybe you better put somethin' on it, George," I said.

"Hell, it's all right." Then he grinned at me. "On second thought, maybe I should. If I went up to the house, maybe that goodlookin' sister-in-law of yours would hold it a while an' fix it up for me, hey?"

I didn't say anything for a minute and he laughed.

"What's the matter, kid, didn't you think she would? Or maybe it's that you don't go for the idea? Is that it?"

"It ain't that," I said. "I never thought about it is all."

"If you ain't, you're a bigger fool'n I thought you were. Hell, everybody else is thinkin' about it, why not you?"

"It ain't none of my business, that's why. She's Johnny's wife," I said, turning away. But I wondered who he meant by everybody else. The only one I could think of was Red Beazly.

George went to talking, though, kind of to himself. "Course it ain't none of my business. An' I'm damn glad it ain't. Johnny's a pretty husky boy, and he gets mad awful easy. If I was to get ideas like other guys I know, I'd be a little worried. 'Course I ain't got the guts some people got." He laughed. "Maybe that's why I ain't rich or famous." He paused for a second. "Or got ideas about Stella, either."

I turned back to him then all of a sudden. "Who's got ideas about her?"

"Why, ain't you one of 'em?" he said, kind of laughing.

I tried to laugh too, but it didn't come off. "Who has, George?"

He turned back to the car then and made like he was examining the motor for a minute. "Johnny dropped me off at Red Beazly's on the way in this morning with his heap. Good thing he didn't come in."

"What's that got to do with it?" I got kind of scared.

"I was talkin' to the bartender. He's an old friend of mine."

He was horsing around on purpose just to make me nervous or mad, so I just waited like it was nothing.

George turned towards me then and leaned on the fender. "He was tellin' me about a babe Red was drinkin' with. An' went out with, a while before. A real dish." He nodded toward the house. "The description fits. Red knows how to pick 'em, too."

"That wasn't Stella. She was home here all evenin'."

"The description fits, kid. 'Course I didn't tell Johnny." He turned again and bent down to look at the motor. "Bring that light over here so's I can see how to fix the next one. An' be a little careful this time, will you?"

I brought the light over and held it so's he could see, and I made sure I wasn't going to bump anything, but the way I felt it's a wonder I didn't. I didn't know what to say, 'cause I figured George would be sure to tell Johnny, and I knew Johnny'd believe him, no matter what.

"Gimme that punch, kid. The number three. An' the hammer."

I gave him the punch. "I'll have to get the hammer out from under the car."

"Okay. But hurry it up. We ain't got all year."

I got the hammer and gave it to him, putting it right in his hand like he told me to do, and I watched him while he hit three quick hits on the punch. Then he straightened up. "That takes care of that one. No way of tellin' it was changed less you use acid." He wiped his hands again on the rag. "It's a good thing I ain't a brave guy, kid, or a troublemaker, or I might say somethin' to Johnny. But I don't aim to be in the middle of anything that comes up between him and Red Beazly."

I tried to think of something to say about that, but I couldn't. There was no sense in saying any more about it, I figured. All I could do was hope he wouldn't tell. So I decided to play dumb. "George, what's Red Beazly got to do with our racket?"

"Hell, kid, didn't Johnny give you the word?"

"He never tells me anythin' if he can help it."

"Red Beazly is boss around this whole neck of the woods. If he'd of been around a few years ago, I wouldn't of been in the trouble I was in. He's got connections, an' he's smart. He figures things out. He figured this out, an' put up the dough. An' fixed up the contacts to get rid of the cars. Red's a good guy to know."

"I figured Johnny borrowed the money."

"Sure. You can call it that if you like. From Red."

"Then he's really the boss. We're all workin' for him?"

"It ain't that easy, either. We're all playin' ball, in a way." He turned back to the car again. "Forget it, kid.

It ain't that important. Let's get back to work. Just remember it's good to have a smart guy on your side."

We went back to work then, getting all the numbers changed to agree with those on the title to the wrecked Ford out in the pasture. That afternoon, then, we'd really have to work, tearing the motor out of the wreck, taking it apart to save all the parts, and then smashing the block and throwing it on the scrap pile. That was the part I always hated most, 'cause it was part of my job and it really made me think about what was going on. It was so sneaky, because most of the time the blocks could of been used. Only we couldn't use them like a regular junk yard could do. We had to get rid of the old numbers.

All the while I was holding the light and handing George tools and listening to the sharp hits of the hammer I kept thinking about it. Now I'd hate smashing the block even more than before, now that I knew I was doing it for Red Beazly. That was always my job 'cause it didn't take any brains, George said, swinging a sledge hammer, and I was doing it so's Red Beazly could sit in his place all dressed up and try to take Stella away, making like a big shot and telling her things most guys don't know how to say.

When George finished with the numbers, he stood back to look. "There it is, kid, just like the factory." Then he laughed like he did every time. "Hope I got the right numbers."

I hoped for a minute he didn't. It would make everything easy, 'cause sooner or later the sheriff would come, and that would be it. It would be a mess for a while, and then everything would be over. For a minute I thought of telling George wrong numbers on the next car they brought in. But I remembered Ma and what it would do to her. And now there was Stella. I couldn't do that, no matter what.

"You want to start on the wreck outside, kid, or wait till after we eat? It don't matter to me."

"It don't make any difference to me," I said. I didn't want to see Stella any sooner than I'd have to anyway. I didn't know how things would be or how I'd act. I knew she said she was sorry, but I remembered her shadow, and now I knew Red Beazly was boss, I felt worse.

"Let's get at it, huh, kid?" he winked at me. "I want to get me some sleep after a while. I ain't made of iron like your brother, an' I ain't in no hurry to get rich, either."

We went outside then and worked straight through till we got the motor torn down and the parts hauled inside the barn and put on the racks. I was getting to know motors, at least how to tear them apart, and George let me do a lot of the work. It wasn't so bad, working out in the sun, 'cause I had to watch what I was doing, and that kept me too busy to think. Ma came out once and yelled for me to come and eat, but I didn't pay any attention. I hoped they'd hurry up and eat before we got through, so I wouldn't have to sit across from Stella.

When we got the motor all stripped and was ready to pull out the motor with the chain fall, I was tired. But I felt pretty good. George said I was learning fast, and he was going to tell Johnny that I was getting pretty good. "Maybe he'll give you a raise," he said, laughing.

"I ain't seen any money yet," I said, but I was just as glad although I tried to sound tough. George laughed again, and we got the motor up on the dolly. It sure was hard, and we didn't feel like talking till we got it over to the scrap pile and dumped it on the ground.

"There it is, kid," George said, wiping his face with his greasy old rag. "Take your sledge and give it the business."

"What if I don't bust all the numbers?" I said like I was joking.

"You don't, an' somethin' else'll get busted. You," he said real low.

"Don't worry, George. I'll get 'em all." I picked up the sledge, and George walked away whistling. I didn't like the way he talked, even if he didn't see I was joking. I swung the sledge then, as hard as I could, and kept hitting right at the piece with numbers. Even after I cracked the iron and finally knocked that piece off, I kept hitting as hard as I could, hardly even noticing the sweat that ran down in my eyes. I kept thinking I was hitting Red Beazly and George Hite and the kids at school. Once, for a minute, I even thought it was Johnny.

Finally, I quit because I was so tired and hot I almost fell over. I went over in the shade of the barn to cool off, and I sat down on the bench. For a minute I was too hot to think, and then I remembered what I was thinking when I smashed the block. It was bad, I knew, almost as real murder, but I didn't feel sorry. I kind of wished it was for real. Pretending didn't help, except while you were doing it.

After a while Ma came out and yelled again. I didn't feel much like eating but I figured I'd better go up to the house. As soon as I ate, I'd have to start cleaning rust off of the car so's we could paint it. And I was so tired from smashing the block, I didn't see how I could do it. But Johnny and George'd be mad if I didn't.

Ma kind of smiled when I came in the kitchen. My face and hands still stung from the powdered soap I kept in a can by the pump to cut grease, and I didn't smile back.

"You certainly been workin', son. You ought to quit in time to eat."

"We was in the middle of a job we had to get through."

"I kept the stuff warm. Leftovers, mostly." She started to dish some stuff out of a pan. I sat down and watched. I didn't feel hungry. But Ma put the stuff on my plate, so I pretended I was. I didn't want to make her fret.

"One of these days I'll take a walk down an' see what you're doin'."

"There ain't nothin' to see, Ma. Just junk cars we're tearin' apart," I said as quick as I could. "It's awful dirty an' greasy. I laughed. "Look at my clothes. You'd get all messed up."

"I guess I been dirty before," she said, and I thought she was through, but after a minute she looked at me again. "I never knew there was so many old cars around. An' Johnny keeps draggin' home more. The pasture'll be full the way he's goin'. What you goin' to do with 'em all?"

"We got to build up a stock, Ma, so we'll have the parts folks want. There's lots of kinds we ain't got yet."

"They must cost an awful lot of money, don't they, son?"

I chewed my food slow for a minute, not knowing what to say. But Ma kept looking at me, so I answered, still chewing my food. "Not so much as you'd think, Ma. Most folks are glad to get rid of 'em if Johnny tows 'em away. But he's got to keep lookin'. Every other junkyard man is doin' the same. Cars is hard to find, an' we've got to have 'em for the parts."

Ma didn't say anymore, and I hoped I told her the right thing. She looked at me once like she was going to ask something else, but then she didn't. I was glad when she got up and went over to the stove. In a minute she brought me a piece of pie, apple, one of my favorite kind. I was still afraid she was going to ask some more questions, so I ate it as fast as I could and then got up to go.

"Is George Hite goin' to be workin' with you this afternoon?" Ma asked as I got to the door.

"No, Ma. It's just cleanin' up I can do myself."

"I wish Johnny'd got some other partner. I can't help rememberin' he's been in trouble. Don't you listen to him, son."

"I won't, Ma. But George is all right. He sure knows cars, an' that's what we need." I went on out before she could say any more. She made me more nervous than George.

I went right on down to the barn even if I didn't feel like it. Things were getting so mixed up I didn't know what to think. It was getting so all the time I was nervous, afraid I'd say the wrong thing. Ma was pretty smart, and so was Johnny, and I was right in the middle. And there wasn't anything I could think of to do except what I was doing. I knew that wasn't good enough, but I couldn't think of anything else. All I could do was lie as much as I could, and hope everybody believed me. It was getting so I couldn't of told the truth if I tried.

I sat on the bench by the barn for a minute, trying to figure it out. But all I could think of was to keep on lying. Lie and lie and lie and sooner or later, the sheriff. Maybe I could talk to him when he found out. But I knew he'd just lock me up with the rest. I went back in the barn then and started to sand down the rust on the Ford. It was all I could think of to do. As long as I kept working with no one around, at least I didn't have to lie.

Chapter 19

Johnny never said anything about Stella being out that night, he didn't even ask, so I don't suppose he ever knew. He was pretty busy anyway, on the go all the time he wasn't sleeping or eating, so we didn't get much chance to talk anymore. I was just as glad of that because he had a way of making me mad so that I'd say things I didn't want to say. And I didn't want to tell on Stella, no matter what. I was sure glad that George didn't tell him. There wouldn't of been much I could say if he did.

Three or four days later, though, I thought sure he knew. He was kind of jumpy all through supper, getting up to look out the window once in a while, and then he said he wanted to talk to me after. I said okay, but I was kind of scared. I figured then that he knew. I wouldn't give Stella away though for anything. I made up my mind to that, and then I felt some better.

By the time I finished, he was already down and standing outside looking down the road. I glanced at Stella, kind of smiling so she'd know I wouldn't say anything, but she didn't even look at me, so I went outside. Ma looked up kind of funny, I thought, and then I figured I was just jumpy.

Johnny looked at me and grinned when I came out. "Feelin' brave tonight, kid?" he asked me.

"I don't know, Johnny. Why?"

"That Goddamned Hite was about half-crocked this afternoon and it don't look like he's goin' to show up. If he does, he won't be a damn bit of good."

"What do you want me to do?" I knew, but I asked anyway. It gave me time to think what I would tell him.

"Somebody's got to drive. And you might's well. I can't do everythin' myself."

"What do I have to do, JHohnny?"

"Just drive the truck, that's all. Just drive an' keep your eyes open an', for God's sake, don't cross me up."

The idea scared me and I wasn't sure what to say. I was in it, sure, but I didn't like the idea. Johnny looked at me again then, kind of sarcastically.

"What's the matter, kid? No guts?"

That did it. "I got plenty of guts," I said.

"Okay then. How about showin' some of 'em? We got a lot of territory to cover tonight, an' there's no use standin' here braggin' about it."

"Okay," I said. "I'm ready. Let's go."

He sure sucked me in right, I thought as we walked down toward the truck. Johnny was smart, at least as far as getting me to do what he wanted was concerned, and I was dumb enough to let him get away with it. I didn't think about that too much, though. I was too scared and excited and everything to think about it.

While I got in and started the motor, Johnny went in the barn for a minute and came out with a pasteboard box about the size of a cigar box. He put it on the seat and got in. I wondered what it was, but I didn't ask till we got out to the road. Then I glanced down at it.

"What you got in the box, Johnny?" I asked as easy as I could.

"Tools," he said. "You behave all right tonight, an' I'll teach you how to use 'em."

"What kind of tools?" I had a pretty good idea. He must of used them to start cars with.

"I'll show you later. Depends on how you act." He lit a cigarette then and threw the match on the floor. The window was right there and he could of thrown it out, but he didn't. The floor was full of butts and matches and stuff, and it used to be clean. That seemed like a long time ago.

"Where we goin', Johnny? Into town?"

"Maybe we ought, and try to find Hite, but we don't have time."

"Where we goin' then?"

"Nashville. You know the way?"

I nodded. It was a town quite a bit bigger than Titus, about forty miles east of us. I didn't think we'd go so far. I glanced down at the gas gauge.

"We got to get some gas, Johnny."

"Get some."

"I ain't got any money with me."

"I'll pay. Wait till we get on the other side of town though."

"Okay." I wondered why but didn't ask and Johnny didn't say. We didn't talk much after that all the way. There was a lot of things I wanted to know, but I figured Johnny'd just think I was dumb or scared or something. I was, but I tried not to show it. We got gas at a station on the highway, and Johnny paid, and we went on. It was a nice night and after a while I forgot what we were out for. It was pretty country and I never got much chance to go east. Every once in a while, though, I'd think about going out and really stealing a car and it'd spoil things for a while.

When we got on the edge of Nashville, Johnny sat up and started to tell me where to go. it was still daylight, and I didn't like that, but he said to forget it. We drove around quite a bit, up one street and down the next, and every once in a while, when Johnny saw a car parked anywhere like one we had in the pasture, he'd write down the street on a piece of paper. When we saw four, Johnny said that was enough for a while, and we went out to the highway to a truck stop. Johnny had beer and I had two cups of coffee and we sat there quite a while, not talking much, just killing time.

Johnny seemed kind of worried, now that we were just sitting, and I guess I showed I was, too. He leaned on the table then and looked at me, half-grinning.

"Kind of excitin', ain't it, kid?"

I nodded. "Yeah. I guess it is." I was more nervous than excited, though.

"That's the best part. It makes you feel like you're alive. Think of all the poor slobs runnin' a Goddamn machine in a factory someplace. Hell, you should know, kid. You had your share of that."

I didn't answer because I wasn't so sure. I kind of liked it. You did your work and you could think. And you didn't have to worry about the sheriff coming.

"I just hope Hite doesn't shoot his mouth off or flash a lot of dough around town. If he does, I'll kill 'em."

That was what was bothering him, I figured then, and it bothered me, too. I wished he hadn't mentioned it. It was bad enough thinking about stealing a car, but now this. George Hite liked to show how tough and how smart he was. No telling what he might do.

"Johnny, maybe we better forget about it for tonight."

"You ain't scared, are you, kid?"

"No, but what if he tells somethin'?"

"He knows better. He ought to. He knows what it's like to get sent up."

"What if he does, though?"

"Forget it, kid. They got nothin' on us." He drank the rest of his beer and then got up. "Come on, kid. We may as well get it over with, even if it is a little early yet. Hell, people are stupid. You can get away with anythin' if you got guts enough."

I waited while he paid, and then followed him out, but I couldn't forget it. What if the sheriff was waiting when we got home? He'd have plenty on us, no matter what Johnny said. Having plenty of guts wouldn't do much good then.

Outside, it was getting dark, but Johnny said there was still too many people on the streets, so we drove around some more, through the main part of town and around through a park that ran by a river. It was nice riding around on a summer night, and I liked to see the people walking around or sitting in the park talking, taking it easy. I mentioned it to Johnny, but he didn't answer, just sat and smoked, not even looking around, just killing time till he figured it was okay to do what he'd come for.

We stopped in a place and both had coffee and then Johnny said it was time to go to work. He said it so easy, like we were going to a shop or store or something. It was hard to believe we were going to steal a car. It didn't seem real, even while I waited till he paid and then followed him out.

When we came out of the place, he took the piece of paper out of his pocket and held it up in the light so he could read it. Then he said, "Let's go, kid," and we got in the truck.

He told me how to get to the street he wanted and to drive slow. I did, and we passed the car that he picked. He had me drive around the block twice, and he looked around, at houses and at the car. Finally he told me to pull up behind it and turn out the lights. It didn't seem real, sitting there in the dark behind the car we were going to steal.

Johnny took some wires and a pair of pliers and a flashlight out of the box and held them up so I could see.

"Here's the tools, kid. Simple, huh?" He laughed and then said, "Follow me when I get it started."

He got out of the truck. I watched him go up to the car. He looked around a minute and then got in. I couldn't see him inside and I couldn't see any light, even though I watched pretty close for a while.

It seemed like he was in there a year. I looked up at the house the car was in front of. It was dark, and you couldn't see much, but you could tell that it was something like the car, little and kind of old. And the people were inside, probably asleep, and the guy who owned the car was there, little and kind of old like his house and his car and worked in a factory. And we were outside stealing his car.

I never thought of it that way before, and all of a sudden I wanted to yell to him to look out, that we were stealing his car while he was asleep.

Then I got really scared. We couldn't get away with it. There were people around. Somebody'd seen us and already called the cops. I stepped on the gas without knowing it, and the motor roared. I almost jumped out of the truck, I was so scared. I must of scared Johnny, too, because I saw a flash of light in the car ahead. I felt like a fool, and I knew Johnny'd be mad. But I was shaking and I couldn't help it.

Johnny got the car started then and drove off. I waited till he got about halfway down the block and turned on the lights and then I followed. He drove through town as slow as he could, and I stayed behind, scared someone would notice and we'd get caught. But Johnny wouldn't hurry, and I had to go slow, too.

Finally we got out on the highway and then he really started to go. I had a hard time following and my lights weren't much good, and I wasn't so scared anymore. I had all I could do staying on the road. I felt a lot better when we got to the farm and put the car in the barn. Nobody was up and everything seemed all right. I went to bed soon as we got in, and Johnny did, too. But I couldn't sleep. I kept thinking about the guy we stole the car from. I felt pretty lousy. I'd rather been back at the box factory even if it wasn't exciting.

Chapter 20

Things really started to pick up in the junkyard.
Johnny started putting ads in the paper, and we had as
much work as we could handle. Even Pa puttered
around once in a while, trying to take care of all the
people who came in for parts. I had to do most of it,
though, as well as work in the barn. Seems as if everybody around had an old car he was trying to make do
until the new ones started to come through. The rest of
the war in the Pacific was over and the car factories
were getting ready to make them as soon as they could
get the stuff, but we didn't pay much attention. We
were too busy. Besides, the longer it took them, the
better it was for us, Johnny always said.

George Hite and me were putting in twelve or fourteen hours a day in the barn, and we even rigged lights
to work in the evening. Johnny was on the go all day
and half the nights, buying up wrecks that nobody
could make do anymore, picking up cars thirty or forty
miles away for me and George to work over, and then
delivering them to Toledo after we got through.

George Hite went with Johnny every night after that
one when I helped him, driving my truck, when they
went out looking for a car to match one of our junkers.
He didn't ask me to go again for a long time, and I was
just as glad. He told George Hite about it though, and
they laughed. I didn't mind too much except that it
made me think of what we were doing. For a while
every time I came near George, he would blast a horn
on a car or gun the motor if it was running. After a

while he got tired of it and I didn't think so much about it when I was working. Once in a while, though, I'd dream about it and then wake up scared.

One thing, though, we had plenty of money. After a couple of weeks I had my cigar box full, and every time Johnny'd give me some more, he'd look at me and say, "Goin' back to the box factory, kid?" I never answered that, though, because at least I could spend the money I got there, and Johnny wouldn't let me spend any of this except for things like a new pair of Sunday shoes or a tire for the truck. He said we had to go easy, that people'd talk. I guess he was right, but money in a box ain't much good to anybody.

In the evenings for a while, I'd get out the catalog and figure out things that I'd buy whenever Johnny'd let me. It was fun for a while, but it was no different from what I did before, and the fun wore off fast. I wished I was back at the box factory or anyplace where you didn't have to be afraid. But then I didn't have money. It didn't make sense. I shoved the catalog under the couch where I wouldn't see it any more. The money or nothing seemed real anymore. Nothing except work and being greasy and painty and tired. But Johnny wouldn't let us slow up, 'cause he said it wouldn't last forever and we had to get ours while the getting was good.

You could see Johnny change almost from day to day. he got skinny and around his eyes was dark and he didn't laugh anymore, not even in the nasty wayt he'd brought home from the army, and it got so nobody in the house talked any more than Ma. The only time I saw Johnny grin like he used to was when two fellows came down from Toledo with a car for us to work over. They said we turned out a good product, and Johnny laughed and said we aimed to please.

I didn't see Stella any more than I had to, only at meals and once in a while in the yard, and then I didn't talk much, mainly 'cause I guess I was still a little mad. She hardly talked to anybody, except to Johnny, and sometimes I'd hear them arguing till late on the nights he was home. The other nights she'd go for long walks, coming in late without turning on the kitchen light, like she didn't want to wake me. But I was usually awake, thinking about the money in the cigar box and how maybe if I ever got enough I could take her away where she might laugh and talk again and not want to go for long walks alone. But I never said anything to her. I'd pretend to be asleep.

Sometimes I tried to figure it out, while I was working or laying on the couch at night, and I'd take all the pieces and try to make something out of them, but I never got very far. None of it made sense and yet somehow I figured maybe it would if I thought about it hard enough, and then I'd fall asleep or Stella'd come in or I'd hear Pa snore or Ma cry out in her sleep and then I'd be back where I started. And the work went on and that was the only real thing in that whole summer. Everything else seemed like something happening in the movies that you know couldn't happen even if it has got you almost fooled for a while. You'd go outside and it'd still be kind of daylight and your eyes'd hurt for a while, but it'd be over. But I knew it was all real, no matter what.

Chapter 21

Johnny always liked to have the masking tape and papers and old rags cleaned up as soon as we finished working over a car, and that was part of my job. I didn't like the smell of paint, but I got used to it, and I liked to pile the stuff up in the pasture and watch how quick and how hot the flames were and how soon they were gone and there was nothing but fine gray ashes. It was the best part of the job. The fire got rid of the mess quick and clean and the wind scattered the ashes.

One afternoon, after we'd finished a job and George Hite'd gone off somewhere with Johnny, I piled the stuff up like I always did and then went up to the house for a match. Johnny wouldn't let us have any in the barn on account of all the paint and stuff around. It was kind of a pain in the neck, but it was a good idea, I guess. There was no sense taking any more chances than we had to.

When I got up near the house, I heard Stella yell out something. She sounded scared or mad, not like her at all, and I started to run to see what was the matter. As I got to the door, she yelled out again. She was yelling at Ma.

"I didn't bargain on this, and Johnny knows it. If I want to go out, it's my business. As if going for a walk was a crime."

"I didn't mean it that way. I only meant . . ." Ma's voice was patient and kind of low, but Stella didn't let her finish.

"Then for God's sake, stop needling me about it. If Johnny doesn't like it, let him say so. As you like to remind me, I'm his wife. Maybe that's wrong, too."

"Maybe it is," Ma said. "Maybe that's the whole trouble. Or one of the troubles."

"Oh, for the love of Mike." Stella ran out past me then without even seeing me and let the screen door slam behind her. I was glad she didn't see me because I didn't want her to think I was listening. And I felt sorry for her, too. I know how Ma could be when she got an idea in her head. Still, Stella had no business yelling at Ma like that. Ma was all right if you knew her. She'd do what she thought she had to, even if it killed her. She was like that, that's all.

I stood outside the door for a couple more minutes and then I went in. Ma was at the table, mixing something in a bowl, and she looked up when she heard me. You could never tell anything from Ma's face. It was always the same.

"Hello, son," she said and kept on mixing.

"Hi, Ma. I came in for some matches. I got to burn some stuff."

"You know where they are, but be careful."

"Don't worry, Ma. I watch the wind all right."

"You watch yourself. You got paint an' grease on your clothes."

I got the matches off of the shelf and started to go out. Then I stopped. I wanted to say something to Ma to let her know everything was all right, but I didn't know what. I thought how she'd feel if she knew what all we were doing. It hit me all of a sudden.

"What's the matter, son?" Ma stopped mixing and was looking at me.

"Matter? Nothin', Ma. Nothin's the matter."

"I guess you saw Stella run out?"

"Yeah, I saw her." I tried to be funny. "She was sure in a hurry. Hope she made it."

"Don't talk that way." Ma's voice got sharp.

"I didn't mean anythin', Ma."

"Well, don't talk like you do." Her voice dropped and she started to mix again. I walked over to the table.

"What you makin', Ma?" I knew she liked me to ask, but the way I felt, I didn't even care, but I looked down at the bowl of dough on the table.

"Makin' some pies for supper."

"What kind, Ma?" I tried to sound like I used to when I was a kid.

"Apple. The kind you boys like. I hope Johnny stays home long enough to eat it."

"If he knows you're makin' apple pie, he will."

"Maybe so. JHohnny doesn't much care about things like that anymore. He's always chasin' around."

"He's been awful busy, Ma."

She knocked some of the dough off of the spoon and then put it down before she answered.

"He's been too busy. He ought to think of other things, too." She stopped a minute and then looked at me. "I suppose you heard me an' Stella argue."

"I heard Stella, Ma. You didn't argue, though, really"

She wiped her hands on her apron. "I don't know what a body's supposed to do. You say things an' then you wonder. It don't do no good to talk. It takes more

165

than that, I guess. Talkin' just don't do no good. But I don't know what else would."

"It'll be all right, Ma. Stella'll cool off."

"That ain't what I meant." She started to spread flour on the table to roll out the dough. I wanted to go, but I didn't know what to say, so I watched. Ma always moved quick. Her hands knew just what to do. I knew what she meant. It went for Johnny and me more than for Stella, and I felt pretty lousy.

Ma must of felt pretty low, too, but she never showed it, just went on making her pies. I wished I could think of something to say, but like she said, talking don't help. Finally, she looked up at me and brushed hair out of her eyes with the back of her hand.

"You better go out an' burn your stuff 'fore it blows all over."

"Yeah, Ma, I guess I better." I went outside then, wishing I could of said something. But no matter what I said, it would have to be a lie, and that wouldn't help.

Some of the stuff had blown around, and I threw it back on the pile. Then I lit it and stepped back. It sputtered a minute and then flames shot up all over. Paint and turpentine sure made a fire, but it was all over in a minute and then there was hot ashes that the wind blew around. I wished I could do that way, let everything go up in a flame and let the wind blow the ashes. Then we could start all over and make things happen different. But that was kid stuff, Sunday School talk, and it just couldn't happen.

As I went back in the barn, I looked up toward the house and saw Stella going in. I hoped it would be all right, but you never could tell. I felt sorry for both of them, but what could I do? I went inside the barn and cleaned up our tools. It was hard getting the paint off, and I didn't think about things so much while I was doing it.

Chapter 22

It was almost dark, and I was sitting in my truck by the side door, fiddling with the gearshift and listening to Bill Glen's tractor down the hill. He farmed and made it pay and his own land wasn't much better than ours, but he farmed his and ours both. He was getting in hay, and I could almost smell it and I was full of the restlessness that Pa called the fidgets that I always got in September. I wanted to talk to somebody, but there was nobody around but Ma and Pa.

There was really a lot I could do--go in and look at the catalog or go into town to a movie or go down to the bowling alley or the poolroom and stand around and drink a couple of cokes and maybe play a game of pinball. There was really not a hell of a lot to do around in Titus. I backed the truck around and drove down the lane. Instead of going toward town, I turned the other way, the way Stella went walking a little while before.

It smelled good out, and I drove slow taking it all in and watching beside the road. I thought I might see her. I wasn't mad at her anymore. It kind of wore itself out. Even though we still didn't talk much, mostly 'cause there was nothing to say, I kind of thought that on a night like that, Stella might want to talk to somebody, and I wanted to tell her Ma was all right. You just have to know her.

Stella was standing back from the road, about a mile from the house, where an old mud crossroad ran back to the river. I slowed up and stopped in front of her.

She seemed a little scared at first, and then she walked over to the truck. She had on a bright sweater and a skirt and a jacket thrown over her shoulders.

"Hi," I said as she came close.

"Hi,Bobby." Her voice sounded kind of tired, and she didn't make any effort to seem glad to see me. I wished I hadn't stopped. She could of at least smiled.

"Restin'?" I asked, feeling kind of foolish.

"Yes. Just resting." She was standing about three or four feet from the window as though she was afraid to come any closer. She looked like a kid.

"I was just going for a ride somewhere. You can ride along if you like," I said as easy as I could.

"No, I'd better not." She looked around quick, as though she was looking for somebody, and she took a step backward. "I . . . I'd rather walk, Bobby." She smiled then. "It's more healthy, you know." There was a funny tone in her voice as she said that, and I figured she was probably still mad at me or afraid Johnny would find out or something. "Girls can get in lots of trouble going for rides." She smiled at that, but it didn't sound funny the way she said it.

I fiddled a little with the gearshift. Suddenly I wanted to get away from her as fast as I could. Right then I wanted to get away from everything and get the truck out on the road and never stop and never look behind me. I just wanted to drive as fast as I could and as far as I could, but at the same time I knew I'd never be able to.

"Okay, Stella," I said. "If you'd rather walk . . ." I hit the last word kind of heavy because I suddenly got an idea of what was going on. She blushed a little, I thought, but it was getting so dark that I wasn't sure. I let the clutch out and left her standing there beside the road. I kept watching her in the rear mirror, and I drove slow so I could.

I didn't want to watch her 'cause I didn't want to know for sure, but I did and then I saw the big car come out of the crossroad and stop and she got in. I'd seen it around town a lot. It was Red Beazly's.

In a minute they passed me, going like a shot, but I couldn't help seeing Red smoking a cigar and looking sporty with his elbow out the window and Stella sitting close to him. Neither of them looked around, and then all I saw was twin tail lights and then they went over a hill and was gone.

It was like everything else. It didn't seem real. It was easier to believe that it wasn't, but I knew that it was. And I knew that I had to do something, but I didn't know what. So I just drove around and it got darker. I forgot to turn on my headlights until some car honked at me as it passed. Finally, when it was good and dark, I just happened to drive over past Red Beazly's roadhouse. Red's car was parked by the side. I drove on past and then turned around and came back. I pulled up and parked near the front.

Chapter 23

I don't know why I stopped there, I wasn't really figuring on going in or anything, especially if Red Beazly
and Stella were in there, sitting at a table and drinking
or dancing and then going over to stand by the juke
box, and Red with his arm around Stella. I sat there for
a while thinking about it, and the more I thought about
it, the madder I got. I could almost see Stella looking
up at Red like she'd looked up at Johnny and even at
me sometimes, laughing at things that weren't really so
funny. It wasn't fair, I thought, and got even madder.
Neither one of them had any right to do things like
that.

Without even thinking about it or thinking what I
was going to do or say, I got out of the truck and went
up to the front door. There was loud music coming
out, even though you couldn't see many lights. It
sounded like people was having a good time. I heard a
woman burst out laughing as I went in the door. It
wasn't Stella, but it hit me almost like it was. I stopped
and almost turned around, but then I went on in.

There were lights just at the bar and the juke box
like before, and I couldn't see too well who the people
were; mostly they were just shapes that you could tell
were men and women, but that was all. It was hot inside, and kind of damp feeling, like along the river
under the trees. I stood just inside the door for a minute, not seeing anything of Stella or Red, and I felt
kind of foolish. My getting mad was just about over

'cause I felt like people were looking at me even if I did know they weren't.

I saw some guys over in the corner then, playing the pinball machines, and I walked over, not to watch them like they'd probably think, but just so's I wouldn't have to sit at one of the tables or just stand there by the door.

One of the games was kind of complicated, with lots of lights and traps and a loud ringing bell. I would of had a good time watching most other times, but I had other things to think about. I should go on out, I knew, but now I was in I had just as much right to be there as Stella. More, even. So I moved around so's my back was to the wall and it would look like I was watching the game. All the time I was looking around the room, trying to figure out who the people were. I hardly heard the bell ringing and the loud crack the machine made and the yells when the guys won a game. i was kind of afraid of what I was going to see, but I kept on looking around.

After I stood there a while, acting like I was as excited as the rest of the guys, I could pretty well make out what the people at the tables looked like. But I still couldn't see any signs of Stella or Red. I was feeling kind of nervous, just standing there, anyway, and I figured I'd better go home. Still, I just stood there, looking around, trying to see who the people were who were dancing. None of them looked like Stella or Red, but it was too dark to tell for sure.

I thought the hell, then, and started to go around the pinball machine so"s I could go out. It was none of my business, anyway, what they were doing, only

Johnny's and it served him right. Stella was just afraid of getting like Ma. It'd be Johnny's fault if she did. I took one last look around the room.

There was a door over in the far wall, at the end of the bar, and as I looked over that way, it opened. A woman came into the room and right after her, a man. I couldn't see who they were, but right away I could tell it was Stella and Red.

I thought they were looking right at me even though I should of known they couldn't see me in the dark, and I turned around quick to look down at the pinball machine. I stepped on a fellow's foot and he gave me a look and a little shove.

"What the hell's the matter, can't you see where you're goin'?"

"I didn't mean it," I said. "I just didn't look." He looked pretty mean, and I backed away. I hoped he wouldn't start anything. But he gave me another nasty look and then turned around again to watch the game. I was afraid to go too close then, so I went around by the wall again where I was before. I kept looking down, though, even if I didn't watch the balls.

After a minute I looked up, like I was tired of the game. Stella and Red were standing over by the bar, talking to a man. I could see them real plain. They were laughing like something was funny. They turned away from him then. I looked back down at the machine, hoping they wouldn't see me. I wished I'd of gone home.

The fellows at the machine called the girl waiting on tables over, and I had to kind of look away while they ordered beer. Stella and Red were coming over, almost as if they were going to come right over to me. I just watched them, figuring if they saw me, there wasn't anything I could do. But they stopped at one of the tables, so close I don't see how they could of helped seeing me. But they didn't even look. Red pulled a chair away from the table, and Stella sat down real nice, smoothing out her skirt, and looking up at Red. He kind of pushed her chair up to the table easy, bending over low like he was whispering in her ear. It all looked so nice, I wished I could of done something like that. But I never even thought of it before. The only place people did it that i could think of was in the movies. It didn't seem like real people do.

Red Beazly walked around the table kind of slow, all the time looking at Stella. She kept watching him, too, and laughing like she was having a good time. He sat down on the other side and leaned over toward her. Their heads were pretty close together over the narrow little table. They were talking. I had to look away. I wanted to run or to go home or something. I looked down at the game.

The girl'd brought all the guys glasses of beer, and they were standing around drinking and talking, not playing any more. The guy whose foot I stepped on looked at me.

"What's the matter with you, fella? What you hangin' around for?" he said, sounding mean.

I didn't know what to say for a second. "I wanted to play the machine, whenever you guys are through," I said as low as I could.

"It takes a nickel. You got a nickel, ain't you, bud?"
he said. He talked so loud I was afraid Stella couldn't
help hearing but I didn't dare to look.

"Of course I got a nickel," I said, feeling in my
pocket. I had one, and I took it out and put it in the
machine, quick, so's he wouldn't say any more. I
moved over so's I could play.

"A real sport," the guy said and moved in close behind me to watch.

I went ahead and played the game, hardly even
watching what was going on. The lights kept flashing
and the bells kept ringing and I shot the balls one after
another, jiggling the machine once in a while so's
they'd think I was trying. All I could think of was Stella
and Red, with their heads close together. I tried to
look over once, but there was a couple of guys in the
way. All of a sudden then there was two sharp clicks
from the machine. I'd won two games without even
knowing how.

I stepped back from the machine then, glad the
game was over. "Go ahead. You play one off," I said to
the guy.

He looked kind of surprised, but went ahead and
played. I stepped back so's I could see Stella and Red.
They were still setting close. They had drinks in front
of them in glasses with stems, but it didn't look like
they drank any. After a minute they got up and started
to dance. I watched them a while, while the guy won
another game. Stella really could dance, and I had to
admit, so could Red. I kind of wished I was like him.
He was holding her close, and she was kind of leaning

on him. I started to get mad again, so when the guy finished the game, I went back to the machine.

This time I really tried to win, playing as careful as I could. It was hard, but as long as it lasted I didn't have to think about Stella and Red. I lost, though, and didn't even make many points. I usually couldn't win if I tried.

"Let me show you how," the guy said, stepping up again. I backed off without saying anything, and I tried to watch his game, but every once in a while I'd look over toward the dancers. I just couldn't help it, but as soon as I thought what I was doing, I'd make myself look back down at the game.

The guy won again, three games this time, and he looked at me and grinned. "Go ahead. Try it that way, why don't you?"

"You play 'em off," I said. "You won 'em. Besides I'd rather watch."

"Okay. You watch close. It really ain't hard." He started to play again.

I looked away, over toward the dancers. Stella and Red had quit and were coming back to the table. Red was behind Stella, with his arm on her elbow, kind of like he was guiding her. A couple of times she looked back at him. When they got to their table, he helped her with her chair, bending over like before. She laughed again when he must of whispered in her ear. I didn't want to watch, but I couldn't help it. They seemed kind of to fit together somehow. Red knew how to do everything right. When he sat down, he took out a cigarette case and held it out to Stella. It was a pretty case, all shiny there in the dark.

Stella shook her head kind of slow, and then Red said something, still holding the case out. She took one then and put it in her mouth. I was surprised. I'd never seen her smoke. But when Red lit his lighter she bent over for a light like she really knew how. She blew out the smoke, and then sat holding the cigarette out between her fingers like ladies do. It still looked like they do in the movies.

They sat there talking and smoking and sipping at their drinks for what seemed like a long time. I lost track of the guy's games until he turned to me. I noticed then some of his buddies were going over toward the door. They left their glasses sitting on the machine, and were talking.

"We're goin' to take off. I left a game on the machine for you," the guy said to me.

"Thanks," I said. I glanced over at Stella. They were sitting with their heads close together. I couldn't watch any more. Besides, with the guys gone, they couldn't help seeing me if they looked. "I got to go, too," I said. "I'll leave it for somebody else. Maybe he won't have a nickel."

The guy laughed at that. "You're a real sport," he said as he started to go. I followed him over to the door, hoping Stella wouldn't look up. As we got to the door, I looked back. They were getting up to dance again. Red was kind of guiding her like he did before.

The other guys went over to their car, laughing and talking, but all I could think of was how chilly it was out after being inside, and how close Stella and Red always were and how it somehow seemed to fit. Red knew just what to do.

Walking over to the truck, I took my time. I could still hear the other guys laughing and yelling. Even the guy who got mad wasn't a bad guy. They were just having fun. it would of been nice to go along with them.

I walked past Red Beazly's car and stopped to look at it. It was a long, low job with a spare tire mounted on the back. It sure was nice, I figured, a girl or anybody would sure feel like something riding around in that. Suddenly I got a mean idea. I wanted to take a knife and cut up all the leather inside. It would serve him right, having that big car and taking up with Stella. I'd even cut up the tires so's he couldn't drive it at all. That would really fix him. You could hardly get tires at all.

But what would it get me? Or him, or Stella or Johnny or anybody. It was the kind of trick a little kid would pull. I walked on over to my truck. It semed about three times as high and half as long as Red's car. no wonder she'd rather go with him instead of me.

I got in my truck and sat there a while, half hoping they'd have a fight or something, and Stella'd come out and start to walk home. I'd watch her a while, letting her walk, and then I'd pull alongside. She'd give me a smile like she gave Red, and then she'd get in and sit close beside me. But there was no use thinking that way, I figured. Stella knew what she was doing, and they wouldn't fight. And I didn't blame her a bit. Red Beazly knew how to treat a woman, and he could give her things too.

I figured what the hell then, and started back to the farm. It wasn't too late, and I didn't think Johnny'd be home, and Ma and Pa'd be in bed. I took my time, driving slow till it got a little chilly. Then I speeded up a little more. I just hoped Stella got home before Johnny. I didn't mind lying for her anymore, but I sure hated to do it for Red Beazly.

I pulled in the lane and parked up by the house. There was no sense in pulling down by the barn. I couldn't park inside any more, anyway. I sat there a while after I turned the motor off. I didn't feel like going in to bed.

It was funny. I didn't feel a bit mad at Stella, even if I knew it wasn't right. You had to live your life, no matter what, and Johnny didn't seem to care. I didn't blame her a bit. But the more I thought of Red Beazly, the more I hated him. I wasn't mad, I just hated him. Sooner or later the sheriff was going to come, and when he did, I was going to tell him everything I knew about Red. That would show him he was no better than anybody else. And when I got through telling everything I could think of, even lies, as long as it was bad, I'd laugh at him.

After I sat there a while, I started getting scared. What if Johnny came home before Stella? I wouldn't know what to tell him. I was stuck in the middle again. I kind of thought for a minute how it would be if I told Johnny she was with Red, and then I followed him down to the roadhouse. Red would see him and try to joke and be friendly, but he'd be scared, and Johnny would hit him then, a short, choppy punch, and Red would go down. Johnny would look down at him a minute and then spit or kick him or something, and then turn away. Red wouldn't get up till Johnny was gone. And Stella wouldn't look at him any more.

That's the way it would be, I thought, if it wasn't for Stella. But knowing Johnny, it wouldn't stop with Red. And I had to look out for Stella. She knew a lot about some things, but she didn't know how things turn out. If she did, she'd stay away from Red Beazly.

I quit thinking about that then 'cause it was no use, and just sat there a while, watching the stars and feeling the chilly wind on my face. It was the kind of night you can feel fall in the air, the kind of night you like to have somebody around. Somebody you can talk to, somebody like Stella was before when we talked, the kind of person you felt like you knew.

I sat there a long time, just thinking like that, and for a minute it seemed almost like it was true. But there was no use in pretending, it only made you feel worse. I figured I'd better go in the house. But I didn't. I just sat there. After a while I guess I fell asleep.

Chapter 24

Something heavy was holding me but I couldn't bend my head to see what it was. Somehow I knew it was chains and there wasn't nothing I could do about them, and all I could see in front of me was deep black and blinding white that made me want to blink, but my eyes, like the rest of me, couldn't move. And in front of me, a lot bigger than me, was Ma. She didn't say anything; she just stared at me and her eyes were cold but they seemed to burn right through me. That was what scared me more than anything else. She just stood there waiting for me to do something, and there wasn't anything I could do.

Something pushed me then, and I fell down, down for a long time and then I remembered. I was in the truck, parked beside the house waiting for Stella to come back. Somebody was shaking me, and I was scared. There was a car pulled up close behind the truck with the lights out and the motor running.

"Come on, kid. Snap out of it, Goddamnit."

"I'm awake. Take it easy."

"Get this heap out of the way. I got to get this car in the barn."

"Okay." I straightened up in the seat and Johnny closed the door.

"Snap it up."

"Okay." I felt around for the key and started the motor.

"Leave the lights off."

I didn't answer, but waited till he walked back to the car and then pulled the truck up and to the side of the lane so that he could get through. He put the parking lights on as he drove past. The car was a new-looking shiny one with big, bright-red tail lights. I didn't remember any like it down in the pasture, but then I really hadn't looked very hard for a week or so. I'd been too busy, and besides I really didn't much care any more.

As I turned off the motor, I watched the tail lights as they went down the lane to the barn. The doors must of been open because all of a sudden the lights were gone--like the tail lights of Beazly's car, I remembered, and then I got scared, wondering what if Stella wasn't home yet. I didn't have any idea of what time it was, and I sure hoped she had gone in while I was asleep. I felt kind of sick as I sat there waiting for Johnny to come up from the barn.

When he came up beside the truck, he was breathing hard. I could hear him before I could see him, and I waited for him to say something. He stood there a minute like a big black shadow. I was sure he could hear my heart or look through me and see that I was getting ready to lie to him.

"What do you think of that baby, kid?"

"Sure looked nice, what I saw of it."

"It is. Worth a nice piece of change."

"We got one in the pasture like it?"

"No. But this time we can afford to take a chance. They'll fix up a title at the other end. We got to be careful, that's all." He stood there a minute and I could almost feel his eyes on me. "Why don't you go to bed, kid?" He sounded tired and somehow like Pa would sound if Pa gave a damn about anything. "It's pretty late, and we're going to have to get this one out in a hurry. By tomorrow night."

"I fell asleep in the truck," I said.

"You're tellin' me?" His feet crunched in the gravel. "Come on, kid. Let's go to bed."

"Okay," I said and got out of the truck and followed him into the kitchen, wanting all the way to run off in the dark as fast and as far as I could. Yet it all seemed kind of unreal like when you go outside late at night and there's nothing but shadows and stars and sometimes a dim glow way off over the fields.

When we got in I looked away when he pulled the light string and pretended it was too bright for me to see. I didn't want to look at him.

"You should of been in bed hours ago. A growin' boy needs his sleep," Johnny said. I stared at his shadow.

"I guess," I said as I started to pull off my shoes. In a minute he turned way and went into the bedroom. I sat down, on the couch with one shoe in my hand, waiting, not scared any more, but just waiting as he pulled the door shut behind him.

After a minute he came out. I pretended not to notice, and put the shoe down on the floor. As I started pulling off my socks, he came over and stood there watching. I looked up at him slowly.

"Where's Stella, Bobby?" He asked so quiet I could hardly hear him. I looked away and pulledoff the other sock.

"Ain't she in bed?"

"You know she ain't in bed, kid. That's why you were asleep out in the truck. Waiting for her. Where is she?"

"Gosh, I don't know, Johnny. I went for a ride an' when I got back I fell asleep in the truck. I didn't even know she was out."

"You're a damn poor liar, kid." He stepped closer. "An you been real noble. Now you can tell me the truth. Where the hell is she? If she's been playin' around, so help me God I'll kill her." He yelled the last part so loud he almost made me jump, but I had to go on with it.

"She goes for a walk once in a while. That's proba- bly where she is now. Maybe she's lost. Hell, I don't know," I said. "I don't blame her for goin' for a walk." I looked up at him. "The way you treat her, anyway."

He dropped his voice. "Well, why didn't you say so? What am I supposed to be, a mind reader or somethin'?"

"You didn't give me a chance. Hell, you never give anybody a chance. You're good at tellin' but you're sure not much on listenin'." I felt like a rat, but I kept looking at him. It's a wonder he didn't get wise. I don't think I ever lied like that to him before.

"Okay," he said, turning away. "Think we ought to go lookin' for her? Where the hell could she be walkin' at one o'clock?" He sounded kind of worried, and I felt a little better.

I shrugged. "She's your wife. I'd forget about the whole thing an' go to bed. Like you said, we got a big day tomorrow." I started to take off my shirt.

"You don't have to rub it in," he said."Somebody has to tell you Goddamn lunkheads a few things. But if I found out you an' her are cookin' somethin' up, so help me Christ..." He went back into the bedroom and I sat there with my shirt half off, not moving. I felt all churned up and shaky inside.

I sat there a while, thinking and listening and waiting until I calmed down some. I could hear Johnny moving around and finally there was a loud spring noise as though he let himself drop on the bed. I got up then and was unbuttoning the rest of my shirt. As I hung it on the back of the chair, the door opened and Stella came in. She looked at me but didn't say anything. Her clothes looked kind of messed up and she looked sleepy. I couldn't help but notice. I felt like she was dirty and I was, too.

"Johnny's home," I said as low as I could.

"Oh, God." She stopped and looked at the door.

"I told him you went for a walk."

She looked at me like she didn't believe me.

"Tell him you got lost."

"Bobby, I want to talk to you. I've got to talk to somebody. I saw you in there tonight. But I didn't say anything to Red."

"You better go to bed." I tried to sound mad. I guess I did, because she didn't say any more and went into the bedroom. I heard Johnny say something and then her and then I didn't hear any more. As fast as I could, I took off my pants and put out the light. I laid there for a long time, wanting to pray or something. But I only knew Ma's way and I knew that was no use.

Chapter 25

All the next morning while we were working over the car Johnny'd brought in, I was trying to figure out what I should do. If things went on like this, sooner or later everything was going to explode. Johnny would have to find out about Stella and Red. Somebody around town would see what he did, and when that happened, there was no telling what he would do.

The only thing I could think of to do was to go to see Red and tell him to stay away from Stella if he knew what was good for him. It wouldn't do any good to talk to Stella, I figured, 'cause now I knew what she saw in Red and I really couldn't blame her. Besides I didn't think I could talk to her any more. But Red would have to listen. He was in this racket as much as any of us, maybe even more, the way George Hite talked.

I planned it out in my mind just the way I was going to do it. I'd wait till Johnny went off with the car when we finished it and I'd go right over to Red's. And no matter who was around, I was going to tell him to lay off, as mean as Johnny could do it. And then without waiting for him to say anything, I was going to turn around and walk out.

Every time I thought about it during the day, though, I got kind of scared. Red wasn't the kind of guy who would stand there and listen. Then I'd try to make myself quit thinking that way. If I could go out and help steal a car, I could sure as anything tell off

Red Beazly. Like Johnny always said, most things were a matter of guts.

We did a really fast job on the car 'cause Johnny didn't want to have it around any longer than we had to, but we did a first class job anyway. We were getting pretty good. Even Johnny said that. He even worked right along with us, and by a little while after noon we had the car painted. Johnny said the paint would be dry enough by the time it was dark for him to take the car away, and he went up to the house to get some sleep, leaving me to take off the masking paper and clean things up. George stayed around to tune up the motor.

The rest of the time after Johnny left I kept thinking about me telling off Red. I wasn't sure what I was going to say, but it would have to be plenty. I kept trying to make myself feel cold and mean about it, and it was beginning to work. I figured I knew how Johnny felt about things and how he could do them. You couldn't have anything left inside you except hate. And I had plenty of that as far as Red Beazly was concerned.

After a while I got to slamming things around till George Hite looked at me and grinned. He asked me to get him a crescent wrench and I told him to go to hell, he could get it himself. It didn't even sound like me. It sounded more like Johny than he did himself sometimes. I hardly even knew it was me saying it till George started to laugh. I don't think I ever saw him laugh that hard before, and I just stood there looking at him, not knowing what else to say.

"My God, kid," he said after a while. "You're sure learnin'. If Johnny an' me don't look out, you'll be runnin' the racket. You sound like you been practicin' like some of the guys do in the stir sometimes. Hell, kid, I'm your boss, remember?"

I started to say I didn't mean it but then I quit 'cause I knew that I really did and it was about time I started saying and doing what I thought. George Hite laughed again and went and got the wrench for himself. I went on pulling masking paper off of the car and throwing it down on the floor, but not as hard as before. I was beginning to feel a little scared again, even though I was kind of sore at George. I didn't think it was so funny. Then it hit me all of a sudden. The thing that scared me most of all was that Red Beazly would laugh. If he did, I didn't know what I would do. But I had to go through with it anyway now. There wasn't anything else I could do about things, and even if this didn't work, at least I had to give it a try.

When George Hite finished up with whatever he was doing to the motor, he said, "Don't bite off any more nails than you can chew, kid," and went off, leaving me to clean up the mess. I didn't answer him, but I was glad to see him go, and I went on cleaning up the mess and the tools, not scared anymore because I wouldn't let myself think about Red Beazly laughing. Besides, I told myself, I ought to be used to people laughing by now. There was no sense thinking about it.

I piddled around the rest of the afternoon, even cleaning up things we usually didn't clean, and a couple of times when guys came in for parts I took my time getting them, even cleaning up an old Chevy carburetor for one of them. I always like to get parts for people anyway, 'cause they acted like you were somebody and knew what you were doing. It was kind of funny in a way, though. People couldn't see inside to what you were really thinking. Times like this, it was a good thing. Otherwise they'd see what a mess you could get yourself in, even if you didn't know why yourself. It kind of made me feel funny, and I even wondered what they'd do if I suddenly said I'd worked almost all day on a stolen car and now I was fixing to go tell off Red Beazly. It kind of made me feel stronger than they were, like I could really handle Red Beazly all right. But still I felt kind of scared.

When Ma called me for supper, I went up to the house, still feeling kind of scared and yet still feeling strong, like as long as I knew what to do, I could do it. I never felt that way about anything before, and I really felt different. I was afraid they could see it in my face, but I guess nobody noticed. At least nobody said anything. Supper was like it usually was, nobody said much of anything. But I was still kind of scared, especially of Ma, and I didn't look at her any more than I had to. She didn't even notice that, either, I hoped.

After supper I walked down to the barn with Johnny. He didn't say very much, but I got the idea that he felt like I did, kind of scared and excited and yet kind of strong. He was thinking about the car he had to deliver with no title or anything. I kept thinking about telling off Beazly.

When we got down to the barn, Johnny lit up a cigarette and we sat down on the bench outside the door. The sun was starting to go down and it was getting kind of chilly. After a while Johnny looked at me. He looked pretty tired.

"Excitin', ain't it, kid, when you sit down an' think about it. But I don't know if it's worth it. We got a good thing the way we been doin', an' we're stickin' our necks out pretty far this time. We can't afford to slip up."

"Yeah," I said. "It is pretty excitin'. But there's no use goofin' it up." He meant one thing and I meant another, but it was all the same. If only I could be sure I was going to handle it right, without goofing things up. To Johnny I said, "I sold fourteen dollars worth of parts this afternoon. Maybe one of these days we can give up the other an' concentrate on sellin' parts. There's sure a lot of people want 'em." I really didn't think that any more, but it was something to say.

"Fourteen dollars! Hell, Bobby, that's chickenfeed. Split it up and what'd we each have? Coupla bucks apiece, that's all."

"Yeah, Red Beazly'd take most of that, I guess," I said without thinking.

"Who's been tellin' you things, kid?" He didn't sound mad, though, and I kind of expected him to be. I shouldn't of said it, even so.

"I ain't so dumb, Johnny. I hear things, an' I can figure things out for myself. I'm in this racket, ain't I?"

Johnny got up then. "Don't worry about Red Beazly. I can handle him all right, when the time comes. Remember who's runnin' this show an' who's stickin' his neck out, that's all. It ain't Red Beazly." He gave me a little punch on the arm. "I guess I'll shove off, kid. You want to ride along, see how the other end works?"

"No, thanks, Johnny. I'm pretty tired. Guess I'd better stay home," I said, but the excitement hit me again. I hoped I sounded natural.

Johnny didn't notice, though. "Okay, kid. Whatever you want to do." He started to go in the barn. "Close the doors after I pull out, will you, kid?" He went on inside, and I just sat there, feeling the excitement inside me, while Johnny opened the big doors and backed the car out. He kind of waved at me and then turned it around. he drove kind of slow down the lane so's not to raise any dust in case the paint wasn't clear dry and then turned out on the road.

As soon as he was gone I got up and started back toward the house to get my truck. About half way I remembered the barn doors and had to go back and close them. I locked them from the inside with the big bar that we used and then came out the little door and locked that. I started off again, running this time. I was scared that if I waited any longer I wouldn't be able to do it.

Driving down to Red's though, I kind of took it easy. I was scared again, and for a while I was afraid I wouldn't be able to think of anything to say. But I had to now, and that was all there was to it. The sooner I got it over with, the better. I was glad it was still early, not even dark yet. There probably wouldn't be too many people around and it'd be easier.

When I pulled up in front of the place, I only saw two cars, Red's and another one, parked over by the side of the building. I stopped right in front of the place where the truck would be handy. I cut the motor right away and got out so's I wouldn't have a chance to think about it anymore. I was nervous and scared and excited, but I went right in. I didn't see Red, so I walked right over to the guy who was standing behind the bar washing glasses.

"Is Beazly around?" I didn't say mister on purpose, and I hoped I sounded tough. The guy didn't look up right away like he would of for Johnny, so I figured it didn't go over. Right then I felt like running out of there but I couldn't. The guy looked up then.

"He's prob'ly busy. What you want to see him about?"

"I'll tell him. Is he around or ain't he?" I said, not feeling as mean as I tried to sound when I said it.

The guy reached under the bar and for a minute I thought he was reaching for a club or a gun or something, like they do in the movies, but away off somewheres I heard a buzzer. The guy didn't say anything, just went on washing his glasses, so I waited. In a minute the door beside the bar opened and Red Beazly came out. He looked at the guy behind the bar.

"What's up, Joe? I haven't got a whole lot of time."

"Feller there wants to see you," the guy said, kind of nodding at me. I felt all of a sudden like I was naked.

Red Beazly looked at me then and kind of smiled. "Why hello, Lust. What do you want with me? Is anything wrong?"

"Plenty," I said, still trying to sound as mean as I could.

"You'd better come into my office then," he said, still smiling. It looked kind of forced, though. I hoped he was scared something was really the matter.

"I can say all I got to say right here," I said, but Beazly went back through the door. I went after him.

"Sit down, Lust," he said as soon as we got in, "and tell me the whole story. I'll do what I can. What happened, did Johnny get picked up or something?" He sat down on a couch that was against the far wall and kind of relaxed like a big shot or something. All of a sudden I got mad. I didn't want to, but I couldn't help it when I saw the couch and him sitting on it and remembered Stella coming out of the office with him.

"It ain't about that an' nothin's happened to Johnny," I said as fast as I could. "It's about Stella." Beazly raised his eyebrows and started to say something, but I didn't give him a chance. "I don't know what's goin' on, but you leave her alone, an' it ain't right for you to..." He grinned at me and I couldn't finish right away. "Besides," I said after a minute, "If Johnny finds out, it ain't goin' to be very funny. Johnny don't take nothin' from you or anybody. Things is in enough of a mess without you makin' 'em worse. Besides, Stella is a good kid, but what chance is she got with people like you?" All of a sudden it sounded funny with me talking so loud and I shut up. Besides I wasn't sure what I was saying. Then I tried to start again but I couldn't. It didn't make sense even to me any more.

Beazly laughed then, kind of low, and held up his hand. "Is that all, kid? Do you have it all off your chest now?"

I just stood there. I must of looked like a fool.

"Then you listen to me for a minute. Stella is a big girl. Nobody tells her what to do. She knows what she wants to do and she does it. Don't let yourself think any different because that's the way things really are."

"No, they ain't," I yelled at him. "She doesn't know how things really are. She thinks . . . She thinks things are . . ."

"That's where you're wrong, kid. She does know, and she knows what she's got to trade. She's a pretty smart girl."

The only thing I could think of then was smashing him as hard as I could, to shut him up, and I kind of dived at him, trying to hit him in the mouth. But before I even knew what was happening, he was up and twisting my arm up behind me. The pain was so bad all I could do was try to keep from screaming or something. He held me that way for a minute, but it seemed more like an hour and all I could do was take it.

"Are you calmed down a bit, kid? Enough to listen to the rest of it? You interrupted before I was finished."

I didn't answer. Let him break my arm, I thought. It was what I deserved, thinking somehow I could change things. I should of known better. I would of if I'd let myself really think.

He gave my arm a sharp little twist that made it feel like he was tearing it off and then he let go.

"Well, are you satisfied? Shall I go on without any more interruptions?" He looked at me like I was an idiot.

I just stood there. My arm was getting numb and I couldn't think. I could hardly even hear what he said for a minute.

"Just one more thing and then you can go. Remember Johnny doesn't scare me. No one else does, either.

I admit it isn't the most pleasant situation in the world, but what is? Stella's getting what Johnny can't or won't give her, isn't she? Something you'll never be able to give her either. Remember that." He gave me a little push. "Any time she wants to quit, it's all right with me. But she doesn't want to." He gave a little laugh. "Now get out. Fast. And remember I never want to see you in here again. Not even as a customer. I don't have any time to waste on fools or people who can't mind their own business." He gave me another little push and I went. What else could I do?

I went out through the other room as fast as I could. The guy was still behind the bar, polishing the glasses. He kind of grinned, and I wanted to run, but I kept on walking fast. Let him grin, I figured. I was a fool, like Beazly said, and I got what I deserved. As I got to the door I wondered if he would tell Stella about it. I could almost hear her laugh, but it didn't make any difference. There wasn't anything I could do about it.

I got in my truck and rode around for hours, not wanting to go home or any place else. I rode through a couple of the towns around Titus, trying to think tough, making like I was looking for cars I could steal. But that was like a kid would do after he came out of a movie, and I was a big enough fool as it was. So I quit that and just rode around till I was almost out of gas. Then I headed for home. I didn't know what else to do.

The lights were out in the house when I got there. At least I wouldn't have to talk to anybody, and I was glad about that. I didn't even care if Stella was out with Beazly or not, and all of a sudden I knew I wasn't even mad at him any more. Stella knew what she was doing.

He was right about that, no matter what else. And I knew I'd do the same if I was him. I'd thought about it often enough, even if it was only thinking.

Chapter 26

The only things I knew how to do without goofing
everything up were working and keeping my mouth
shut, no matter what happened, as I figured that was
the only thing I could do, that and keep on waiting.
Sooner or later the sheriff would come and I wouldn't
have to worry any more. It was a hell of a way to have
to look at things, but I didn't know how else to. For a
while I thought about taking the money Johnny'd been
giving me and clearing out. I had quite a little in my
cigar box and Johnny'd given me fifty dollars more
when he got back from delivering the last car. I gave
up that idea pretty quick, though. Running wouldn't
help a bit 'cause I'd be carrying everything with me anyway. You can't run from things in your mind no matter
how far you go or how fast.

I quit worrying about Stella and Red Beazly,
though, and I wasn't even worrying about the car stealing racket like I used to. There was nothing I could do
except wait and keep my mouth shut and work. In a
way, that was the exciting part, just waiting. When people came in for parts I kind of pretended that's all
there was to it, just selling used parts, but that was
habit, I guess, more than anything else. I couldn't
shake that tight feeling that came with waiting, no matter what I did. It was kind of like watching a cat sneak
up on a bird.

A couple of times I felt like talking about it to somebody, but there was nobody who knew the whole story
except me. It got so I didn't talk at all except when I

had to. I was afraid I'd let something slip, especially to Johnny or Ma. I knew they were bound to find out sooner or later, but I didn't want to be the one who told them. I knew what would happen when Johnny found out about Stella and Red Beazly, but I wouldn't even let myself think about when Ma found out about the rest of us.

Stella tried to talk to me once or twice when I was hanging around the house, but I wouldn't listen. I'd always make some sort of excuse and go back to the barn. She acted like she had to explain or say she was sorry or something, but I knew that was no use. I knew what was done was done, and explaining wouldn't make any difference. Besides I kept remembering what Red Beazly said, that he was giving her something I never could, and I didn't want to hear about it. I didn't even want to think about it. I didn't worry about it anymore, but I couldn't help thinking about it. Having her explain it would only make it worse. Besides, every couple of days when Johnny wasn't home she'd still go for a walk in the evening. And then I'd sit around and think about the couch in Red Beazly's office. It made me feel kind of sick.

Johnny never noticed anything about it, and it was easy to see why. All he ever thought about was work, turning out more cars, just like a factory. It wouldn't last forever, he said, and we had to get ours while we could. A couple of times he talked about getting us some help, but he never did anything about it. He didn't want to split up the money any more than he had to. It was just as well, though, I guess. I was so tired most nights all I could think of was going to bed. And I didn't even dream any more.

Then about a week or so after I tried to talk to Red Beazly, I'd just finished washing up at the pump before supper and I couldn't find the towel on the hook. I had soap in my eyes and it really stung, so I hollered for Ma to bring me a towel. In a minute she came out, but instead of just handing it to me, she began to rub my head real hard with the towel like she used to when I was a kid. She hadn't done anything like that in a long time and it felt kind of good, but for some reason or other I didn't want her to do it. I felt kind of funny.

"Give me the towel, Ma. I got soap in my eyes, an' it stings." I shook my head away from the towel and took it from her so's I could rub my eyes. When I got the sting eased off a little and finished wiping my head, she was still standing there. It always made me feel kind of embarrassed when Ma looked at me like that. She didn't do it very often. I turned away and hung the towel on the hook so's I wouldn't have to look at her.

"Soon as things slack off in the junkyard, Ma, Johnny an' me are goin' to start work on the bathroom again. We was talkin' about it the other day," I said just to have something to say. We really didn't though. I don't think either of us ever thought about it much. "It'd be nice, specially in the winter, havin' one in the house."

"It would be nice, I suppose," Ma said, "but it really don't make much difference. It'd cost a lot of money."

"We been goin' all right sellin' parts, Ma. Things are goin' pretty good. I sold two generators an' a fender today. People are gettin' so's they know we got parts now." I hated to talk like that to Ma, not exactly lying but the next thing to it. She looked over at the old cars lined up in the pasture. "We're really gettin' a pretty good stock of parts."

"Son, look at me," she said kind of quiet. I turned around as slow as I could, feeling kind of sick all of a sudden.

"What, Ma?" I tried to sound natural.

"I ain't had much time, I guess, to talk to you since Johnny's been home. I been tryin' to, but things always come up."

"We talk plenty, Ma. Every day, don't we?"

"It ain't that. There's things that I been thinkin' about."

"What, Ma?" I could feel myself getting scared inside.

"I ain't been sleepin' too well nights lately, son. An' when you lay awake, things start to bother you. "Specially when you hear a lot of cars and things late at night."

I made myself laugh at that. "That's natural around a junkyard, Ma. There's cars around all the time. That's your business, cars." I tried to change the subject like it was nothing. "Maybe you ought to go in to see the doctor, Ma. He'd prob'ly give you something to make you sleep." Like he did before, I almost said then, but I didn't let myself. It might make her remember what happened before. "They got pills an' things that make you sleep, Ma."

"Yeah. I guess they have pills that make you sleep, so's you don't hear things at night. But that ain't what I need. There's other things would help a whole lot more."

"Maybe you ought to cut out the coffee, Ma. You drink an awful lot of it. Maybe that's what's the matter."

"It ain't the coffee, son." She kind of half-turned away. "It's . . . I don't know. I just don't know is all." She didn't say any more for a minute, just stood there looking out over the cars in the pasture like I was doing before, but I really don't think she saw them. It was more like she was looking at nothing like she did sometimes when something was bothering her. Ma was like that.

I wanted to say something right then, more than I ever wanted to do anything before. I wanted to let everything run out of me and tell Ma about stealing the cars and about Stella and Red about how I tried but not hard enough or not in the right way or because I was alone and a fool. I had the funny feeling that Ma wanted me to right then, too, that she was waiting for me to tell her everything I'd been thinking about since I was a little kid. I wanted to and I almost did, but I didn't. I couldn't for some reason. Right then I knew I would if I could but I couldn't. I just stood there. If Ma would of asked or even touched me right then, I think it would of all come out because I felt like I was slopping over inside. But she didn't. She just stood there looking out over the pasture at nothing, waiting for me. It seemed like an hour before she turned to me again. her face was in the shadow. I don't know whether I was glad or not that I couldn't see it.

"I guess I better go in an' get supper on the table, son. Johnny said he'd be home, but I don't know whether to wait. Your Pa'll be hungry an' the stuff'll be cold."

"Johnny'll be home, Ma. He knows I need the truck to drive you in to church meetin' tonight. I told him this noon."

"It's all right, son. It don't matter, I guess. I got my ironin' to do anyway." She sounded awful tired, and I could hardly hear what she said. It didn't even sound like Ma.

"It's Wednesday night, Ma," I said. "You always go to church."

"I know, son. I been goin' for years," she said. I was glad then I still couldn't see her face very well.

"Johnny'll be home. I can take you easy, like always."

"It don't matter, son," she said again and then went in the house. She walked straight like she always did, but somehow she looked kind of slumped over. It didn't seem real.

I didn't go in the house, but I stood there for a minute, all of a sudden feeling kind of empty, almost like I had told Ma all those things and I was tired from talking. I sat down on the well cover and my eyes started to sting again. I rubbed them a while and finally they quit. I just sat there, I don't know how long, not even thinking, just feeling empty inside. Then Johnny come up the lane in the truck. I got up and started to go inside so's I wouldn't have to talk to him, but he honked the horn quick a couple of times so I turned around and waited. He stopped the truck real sudden, right in front of me, raising up a cloud of dust and then stuck his head out the window as he cut the motor.

"Don't go in yet, kid. I want to talk to you a minute."

The only thing that I could think of right away was that he'd found out about Stella and Red. He didn't act mad, though, so I knew it couldn't be that. The only other thing he ever talked to me about was the car stealing racket, and I didn't want to talk about that or even think about it right then, but I waited anyway. There was no sense in making him mad.

"You ain't got anything planned for tonight, have you, kid?" he asked while he was getting out of the truck. "George Hite is boozin' again, and I really got a litle gold mine spotted. I wasn't goin' to ask you, kid, but I ain 't got any choice. I got to get it tonight." He put his hand on my shoulder.

I kind of moved out from under his hand. I was still thinking about Ma. "I got to drive Ma in to church. It's Wednesday night, remember?" I said, moving away.

"Oh, hell. She can stay home for once, can't she?"

"Not Ma if she can help it. You know her better than that. An' there's no sense in givin' her ideas, is there?"

"This ain't goin' to keep. We got to get it tonight. We got to work somethin' out. Maybe while she's in church."

"I kind of promised I'd go in with her," I said, thinking fast. "I didn't want to go, no matter what. Especially not while Ma was in church." Johnny laughed at that, though.

"Hell, kid are you goin' nuts or somethin'? You don't want to listen to all that crap, do you?"

I didn't want to, but I didn't want to steal a car either. I remembered last time too well. And I could al most see Ma standing there like she was looking off across the pasture at nothing. "I can't go, Johnny," I said after a minute. "Not tonight, anyway. Wait till to-morrow." I figured George Hite would be okay by then.

"Tonight's our only chance. The guy who owns it's away, an' he keeps it in his garage. Any other time he couldn't help hearin'."

"I got to take Ma to church, Johnny," I said, turning away to go in the house. "I can't help it, that's the way it is."

I went on in the kitchen, with Johnny right behind me. Ma was setting the table. Right away I said, "Johnny's home, Ma. I can take you to church like I said," hoping Johnny'd get the idea I'd promised Ma I'd go and was going.

Johnny stepped around the table quick before Ma could answer. "Look, Ma," he said, "Can't you let it go for this once? It ain't that important, an' I got somethin' I want Bobby to do for me tonight."

"I'll take you, Ma," I said real quick, but Ma turned away and went back to the cupboard. She just reached up and took out more dishes like she hadn't even heard.

"Look, Bobby, I can't help it this once. You got to do what I asked. Ma don't have to go tonight."

I started getting mad. "I'm goin' to take Ma. That's all she's got, goin' to church," I yelled at Johnny.

"It ain't that important. This is."

Yeah, stealing a car, I almost yelled, but I quit in time. Johnny made a motion like he was going to hit me and then caught it in time too. We just stood there a minute looking at each other. I almost forgot about Ma being there until she came over to the table with her hands full of cups. She started setting them around, not even looking at Johnny and me.

"I wasn't figurin' on goin' to church tonight, boys," she said without looking up from the table. "Like Johnny said, it ain't very important. Not any more, anyway. It don't make any difference." She didn't even look at us but went back to the cupboard. I just stared at her. It didn't seem like Ma at all.

"See, what did I tell you?" Johnny said. "It's okay with Ma."

"Yeah, Johnny," I said, but I didn't mean it. I was more scared than I'd been before, and not about stealing the car.

Chapter 27

Johnny and me brought the car in, like he wanted, and this time it wasn't so bad. At least Johnny said I kept my head. I wasn't scared even if I did have to wait a long time while Johnny got it out of the guy's garage. When I got a look at it in the barn the next day, I saw why Johnny wanted it so bad. It was a real beauty, a forty-one Chrysler, same model as one a guy'd smashed up down the road and Johnny'd towed home a couple of weeks before. It was worth a lot of money. You could hardly tough good forty-ones like that any more.

We really did a good job on the car in the next couple days. I was glad to have work to do and George Hite to keep riding me the way he did. Whenever we let up I'd start thinking about Ma, standing there waiting for me to tell her everything. Or I'd think about Stella, how she'd look at me once in a while like she wanted to talk. Every time I'd look the other way. I couldn't stand the way her eyes looked like a puppy's that'd been licked for wetting the floor. And I kept seeing her in my mind the way she looked when she came in that one night, messy and sleepy looking. It was a good thing there was plenty to do. it keeps you from thinking.

After we got through working it over and gave it a nice coat of paint, George Hite took off somewheres like he always did, leaving me to clean up. I was taking the old newspapers and masking tape off the car, taking my time and thinking about Ma. I couldn't figure out why she wouldn't let me take her to church. It wasn't like Ma. She believed in going, she believed it was good, that you were on God's side and He was on yours if you went to church. And then she said it didn't make any difference. I couldn't figure it out.

I was kind of thinking out loud, like I do sometimes when I'm alone, and I didn't hear the doors open, but when I looked up, Ma was standing there in the barn. I was surprised, 'cause I'd never seen her down to the barn before, but I just said, "Hi, Ma" and went on working. I knew she had something on her mind, and if she wanted to, she'd say it. If not, she'd just freeze it up inside her until the only way it came out was in the way she looked at you.

She didn't say anything, just stood there for a few minutes watching me as I pulled off the paper and tape and wadded it up in a big ball. She made me nervous, watching like that, and finally I threw the paper down on the floor and turned around. She still didn't say anything and I didn't know what to say.

"Nice lookin' car, ain't it, Ma?" I finally said. "We overhauled it from junk."

"Johnny'll get a lot of money for it, won't he?"

"I guess so, Ma."

"He's doin' pretty well, ain't he?"

"Yeah, he is. We all are. Johnny sure had a good idea startin' this junk yard." I wouldn't look at her and say it, so I kicked at the ball of paper on the floor.

"An he's goin' to get on in the world, make a lot of money, take care of all of us. Maybe even git the bathroom put in the house."

"That's what he says, Ma. I hope he does. Somebody's got to get things done. Like he says, the rest of us got no sense."

"Johnny's like your Pa was." She seemed to be thinking out loud like I do once in a while.

"Only Johnny's tryin' to do somethin' about it."

"Your Pa did, too. He farmed, like a man was meant to."

"Not as long as I can remember, Ma."

She didn't seem to hear that. "An' I tried to help him, however I could."

"Johnny's got Stella. She can help him, Ma."

"Stella!" Ma spit the word out like it was poison."No good, flautin' herself, wearin' tight sweaters an' readin' novels, ruinin' Johnny an' you, too, an' even makin' your Pa . . ." She turned around suddenly and looked out the door and up toward the house. "Out nights, both of 'em, till all hours, chasin' around, God knows what all. An' never together, only in bed, like a couple of tramps." She turned around again and couldn't help but see that I was nervous.

"Son, I'm gettin' kind of old. Not as old as some but older'n a lot, an' I've seen a lot an' tried to do what I was made to do. An' now I've got a Jezebel under my roof. A Jezebel an' a couple of thieves. What in God's name have I done?"

"Ma!" I felt as though somebody hit me in the stomach.

"I've got eyes, son, an' ears. You can't fool me forever."

"Ma, we ain't . . ." It wasn't any use lying anymore so I shut up.

"How long do you think it'll be before the sheriff comes for you? How long?" She sounded as though she was shaking inside and it scared me. I just stood there looking at her, trying to keep away from her eyes.

"An' your brother is out stealin' and she's in there gettin' ready for God knows what, and your Pa is sittin'." She brushed her hair out of her eyes, and I noticed how gray and stringy it was. I had a funny feeling that I was getting a good look at Ma for the first time. I had a feeling that there was something familiar about her from a long time ago, but I didn't know what.

"Ma, I . . ." I looked away.

"It don't help to talk, son. Not now, anyway. It's too late. Maybe it always was." Her voice sounded tired, but different than it usually did, like she knew what I was going to say and how I felt about things. Suddenly I felt sorry for Ma. I don't think I ever really did before. I wished she didn't have to know about the way things really were. But there was nothing I could do. She had to find out sooner or later.

"Things can't go on like this, son. They just can't. I don't know what your Pa or me ever done, but it must of been bad." She pushed her hair out of her eyes again. I wanted to do it for her.

"It ain't anythin' you ever done, Ma. Honest, it ain't."

"Or what we didn't do."

"Or that either, Ma. You done your best. You did anyhow. Maybe Pa didn't, but you did."

"Maybe so, but it wasn't good enough." She looked up toward the house again. I looked too, and Stella was just taking some silk stockings and things of hers off of the line. Ma looked back at me.

"Are you goin' to give it up, son?"

"I can't, Ma. Not now. You know that." I couldn't look at her any more, but I could see her as clear as anything in my mind, and suddenly I remembered the dream.

"You caught it too, whatever it is that gets into men, makes 'em steal an' everythin' like they were dogs goin' after bones."

"No, Ma. If I got it, it's there. I never caught it. But that's not what I mean. I just can't quit now, that's all."

"That's what your Pa said when he was killin' himself workin'. An' he didn't quit til they made him. An' then he quit everythin' an' look at him now."

"Johnny's smart, Ma. You got to quit frettin'," I said, trying to sound a lot more sure than I felt.

"The good Lord is smart, too, son, if you give Him a chance."

"They crucified Him, Ma." I didn't want to argue with her, and I looked away. I couldn't stand the look in her eyes. "He didn't look out for things like Johnny does." I wished I believed it.

Ma said, "They killed Him. Yes, they killed Him, all right, but they didn't stop Him. Maybe that's what it takes. Maybe you got to die to make things come out right."

"I don't know what to do, Ma," I said.

"I know," she said, and then started to walk toward the door. "Better get washed up for supper, son," she said. Her voice was different all of a sudden.

"Okay, Ma." I turned away and rubbed my finger on a dust speck on the shiny paint of the car. I didn't want to watch her leave, and I rubbed the speck as hard as I could, even after it was gone.

I monkied around in the barn a while, not doing anything in particular, and not wanting to go up to the house. I kept saying "Thief" to myself out loud and it didn't sound real. But I know that it was. That's what I was, and nothing I could do now would change it. I could quit like Ma said, but that wouldn't erase it. And sooner or later the sheriff would come. I'd been fooling myself long enough. You believed what you wanted to, whether it was a movie or a catalog or real. I didn't let myself believe what was real before, but now I had to. And I was scared. Not only for me, but for Johnny and Stella and Ma. Mostly, for Ma. It kept running through my mind. Ma knew. Ma knew.

Finally I went up to the house. It was going to be a nice evening, chilly, but clear and nice, the kind of night I always got restless, but I knew I wouldn't tonight. I felt kind of empty inside. I pumped the basin full of water and put it on the bench and went through the motions of washing. I emptied the water out on the grass and hadn't took the towel off of the hook yet when I heard the shot.

It sounded like a cannon going off somewhere inside the house, and for a second I just stood there with the towel in my hand, listening to the rattle of the windows. Then I heard Stella scream and I ran in the house. Stella was sobbing somewhere and there was the sharp smell of gunsmoke in the air. I ran in the parlor, passing Stella in the doorway and bumping her hand, but I didn't stop till I looked in the front room, where Ma and Pa slept. I guess I knew right away what it was.

There was Ma, or what had been Ma, laying sprawled on the bed, looking skinny and little, like an old shirt somebody had tossed there. Pa's old rifle and a yardstick she must of used to fire it with were beside her on the bed. There was so much smoke in the room that you couldn't see her face, and I didn't go any closer. I knew what I'd see. I just stood there in the doorway, looking for a while, and then I went outside.

Chapter 28

Ma had a nice funeral, the best we could give her.
We had it in town, at a funeral parlor that the man
said was the finest in the state, although Pa didn't like
it. As I thought about it while Ma was laying there, I
could see that maybe the man was right, but Pa was,
too. It was no place for Ma or for anybody you cared
anything about. And it was my idea. I wanted the best
for Ma, and the man said that she had it, but it sure
wasn't Ma's kind of best.

One nice thing was the flowers, most of them big
fall flowers, but lots of roses, too. There was a big
bunch of roses I bought myself and the others we just
ordered. The first flowers I'd ever bought Ma, the first
Johnny'd ever bought her, were piled around the best
coffin the man had, and Ma was dressed in gray -- in a
new gray dress that she hadn't had to make for herself.
Everything was the best -- even the flowers and the
card Red Beazly sent -- and it was such a rotten joke
on Ma that I wanted to laugh as nasty as Johnny could.
Ma liked flowers, and now, finally, she had lots of them.

I wanted to yell at all of them -- Johnny, Pa, the
preacher, but mostly at myself because Ma had the
best for her hole in the ground. It was as good as the
movies. Lies that weren't even good lies. I was glad
when it was over, when Ma was under a pile of flowers
and gray-red clay and we went back to the farm and
the undertaker's big black car let us out and went back
down the hill, speeding up like we was vomit it was
glad to get rid of. I felt like we were.

Johnny said something about some coffee, and him and Stella and Pa went in the house. I stood outside for a while, looking down the hill toward Bill Glen's, where the trees still had most of their leaves. Ours were almost down because we were high and caught more of the wind. I just stood there and stared, not knowing for sure what I was going to do.

One thing I did know, I was through with the farm, through with Pa and Johnny and Stella and stealing and everything. I knew I couldn't stand it any more. I had to live with myself and that was bad enough. I didn't know how much longer I could even do that, but I'd take the money out of my cigar box, and I'd run no matter where, as far and as fast as I could.

Johnny stuck his head out the door then and told me to come in and have some coffee. I didn't want to say anything, so I went in. Nobody said much, and it was instant coffee that Stella'd heated water for, so I drank it as fast as I could. Then I picked up my overalls and went in the front room to change. It seemed as though I could still smell smoke in the air, so I hurried up and changed and hung up my good clothes. I had to get out. It seemed like the house was closing in on me.

I went out to the barn. There was no place else to go and I had to figure what I was going to do. It seemed like a year instead of three days since Ma came in and said that talking didn't help, that it was too late for talking.

Chapter 29

I sat down in the forty-one Chrysler we had in the barn and left the door hang open. It was the car I was working on when Ma came in the barn, and it was a pretty car. But I didn't even pay much attention to the bright marble stuff that ran around the inside. I just wanted a place to sit and have a good think, and the car was handy.

When I'd been there maybe ten minutes or so but hadn't done any real thinking, just sat there kind of numb, I heard the barn door open. I figured it was Johnny, come to see about getting rid of the car already, but I didn't turn around to see, and I didn't even move when I saw it was Stella standing by the open car door looking at me. She hadn't changed her clothes, and she was dressed in thin, shiny black.

'Bobby, I'm sorry. About everything," she said as though she meant it.

"Talkin' don't help now," I said, looking away.

"Don't say that, Bobby. Don't freeze all up inside like that."

"Like Ma," I finished for her.

"Yes," she said quietly. "If you want to put it that way. But you can't let yourself. You've got to live, too."

I rubbed my finger over the shiny marble stuff, not saying anything or even letting on I knew she was there.

"Bobby, listen to me."

I kept on feeling the smooth, cool finish.

"Bobby, you've got to be glad she's out of it. At least she's free of all this. Look at it that way."

"What's the use of lookin' at it at all?"

"Don't you think I know how she felt? Good God, I'm a woman. I know how it feels to have things all twisted up inside you till you don't know what you're doing."

"Ma knew what she was doin'. It was the only thing she could do."

"Bobby, listen to me and try to believe me."

"I am," I said. "How can I help listenin'. You're talkin' an' I'm sittin' here, ain't I? Go ahead and talk."

"I know what you're thinking, and I don't blame you. I was a fool for having anything to do with Red Beazly. But that's all over. I was a fool and I'm sorry. Can you believe that?

"Don't answer now if you don't want to," she said after a minute. "But give me a chance. When I leave here I want one person to know why. And Johnny wouldn't understand if I told him."

That sort of floored me and I looked at her. She looked like she was going to cry or laugh, but I wasn't sure which. "You mean you're leavin' Johnny?"

"There's nothing else I can do now, is there?"

"You're his wife."

"That's only a name. I've been called a lot of things, and in two weeks he won't even remember what I look like."

"Johnny loves you."

"No, he doesn't. He acts as though I'm a dirty habit he practices down behind the barn. And it'll always be like that. he's like the rest of you, not able to have a normal, decent feeling for another person without being ashamed of it. That's the real trouble, if you want to know."

"That's not true," I said, but I wasn't sure. Of that or anything else. I didn't know what to think.

After a minute she leaned forward and put her hand on my knee. I didn't move, but looked away.

"I'm sorry, Bobby. I didn't mean that."

"It's all right."

"No, it isn't all right. I don't want you to hate me, too. No more than you do, at least."

"I don't hate you."

"I don't blame you. God knows I haven't done anything to prevent it." She took her hand off my knee. "I guess there's nothing more to be said, is there?" She started to turn away. "Goodby, Bobby."

I remembered Ma turning away like that. "Stella, wait."

She stopped and then turned, half-smiling at me. I didn't know what to say, so I tried to smile. Then as she came back toward me, I said "I believe you, Stella. And I'm glad you're leavin'. There's nothin' here except trouble an' hate. An' I'm leavin too. I don't know where, but I'm goin'." It all busted out of me at once. I wanted to talk. I felt like I had to talk to her. She sat down on the seat beside me, and I kept on talking. I don't know what I said, there were so many things, and most of them didn't make sense, but she listened and smiled and looked at me. When I finally ran down I felt a little foolish, but she put her hand on my knee again. It felt warm and I leanced closer toward her. I felt good, like she was part of me. I never felt that way before with anybody.

"Go ahead, Bobby, tell me more. Talking does help when you've got somebody to listen."

"There ain't much else to say."

"Then just sit until there is." She leaned close to me and kissed me lightly on the lips. It was soft and cool like a leaf falling in clear smooth water, and I felt warm and rested, like I wasn't me anymore. I felt like a fool, but I leaned forward and she kissed me again.

"You little bitch!" Johnny came out of nowhere, grabbing Stella by the shoulder and pulling her out of the car. She let out a little scream and he threw her down on the floor, swearing at her. I felt like I was dumb for a second and then I started to get out of the car. He came towards me then. His mouth was half-open and there was a wild look in his eyes.

"Johnny, wait," I yelled, but he came on.

"You bastard," he said. "You no-good bastard."

I got out as he hit me. I saw stars and I almost fell, but I got away. Stella screamed again, but Johnny came after me. There was no place to run, so I stood there.

"I'll kill you," he kept saying, "I'll kill you."

As he came closer, I yelled, "Johnny! Johnny, wait!" again, but he came on. I saw an iron pinch bar on the floor and grabbed it up. He swung again and missed and as he half-turned I hit him as hard as I could. He crumpled up and fell and Stella screamed again once and then it was quiet.

Chapter 30

I walked down the hill by myself. The nearest phone was at Glen's and I could call the sheriff from there. It was the first time in my life I knew what I was going to do, and I felt calm and clean like after a hot bath, and it was going toward evening. It would be a nice night.

I tried to feel sorry, but I couldn't. I could see Johnny fall and lay there like a pile of old clothes and I could hear Stella cry, but I couldn't feel sorry. It happened, and that was all. I walked slower, trying to figure it out, trying to think what I could of done so things would of come out different, but that was no use either. It didn't make sense. All I could do was call the sheriff and tell him the whole story. Maybe he could figure it out.

ABOUT THE AUTHOR

David D. Anderson, University Distinguished Professor at Michigan State University, is editor or author of thirty-six books and more than three hundred articles, essays. short stories, and poems.

A native Ohioan amd a veteran of both World War II and the Korean War, he has received the Michigan State University Book Manuscript Award for his critical biography SHERWOOD ANDERSON, MSU's Distinguished Faculty Award, Bowling Green State University's Distinguished Alumnus Award, the Society for the Study of Midwestern Literature's Distinguished Service Award, and the honorary degree of Doctor of Literature from Wittenberg University.

He edits *MidAmerica, Midwestern Miscellany,* and *SML Newsletter,* and has lectured throughout Europe, Asia, and Australia. He is listed in WHO'S WHO IN THE WORLD, and WHO'S WHO IN AMERICA.